FOOD FOR LOVE

Following a row with her parents over the use of an unexpected inheritance, Jess Davis rushes off to Cornwall. She stands in for Ben Slater's sick mother and loves running the small tearooms. Soon, her ambitious ideas lead her to suggest expanding the business to become a full restaurant, and she offers to buy a half share. Could the handsome Ben be her motivation or is this really a viable proposition?

CHRISSIE LOVEDAY

◆

FOOD FOR LOVE

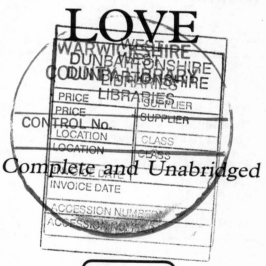

Complete and Unabridged

LINFORD
Leicester

First published in Great Britain in 2004

First Linford Edition
published 2005

British Library CIP Data

Loveday, Chrissie
    Food for love.—Large print ed.—
Linford romance library
    1. Love stories
    2. Large type books
    I. Title
    823.9'14 [F]

    ISBN 1–84395–794–9

Published by
F. A. Thorpe (Publishing)
Anstey, Leicestershire

Set by Words & Graphics Ltd.
Anstey, Leicestershire
Printed and bound in Great Britain by
T. J. International Ltd., Padstow, Cornwall

This book is printed on acid-free paper

1

'What you're suggesting is quite ridiculous,' Ben exclaimed, his face quite implacable.

'But you haven't even listened to what I was proposing. There's so much potential here. We could make this into something really sensational. Put this forgotten place on the map.'

She gazed into the startling, almost honey-coloured eyes. He was exactly like every dream of her ideal man. How could she be attracted to a man who scarcely seemed to have noticed her? Not as a person. He was grateful enough for her ability.

'Jess, I do understand what you're saying. But it isn't my place to start knocking down my own mother's . . . well, café. It really is no more than that. It's a seaside café, pure and simple.'

'Precisely. It's a place for the town's ladies to eat scones and jam. It could so easily be a proper restaurant. We could get the same sort of reputation as that TV chef bloke along the coast. We could use the same suppliers and I have certainly got enough catering skills and imagination to compete with the best.'

'I'll grant you that all right,' Ben replied with a smile. 'Plenty of imagination. Trouble is, you haven't got the money to go with the enthusiasm.'

He glanced at the extraordinarily pretty girl standing before him. Her dark hair flicked over her shoulders and the dark eyes burned with the sort of passion he'd almost forgotten existed.

'Oh, but I have . . . '

She bit her lip. She had nearly given herself away. She'd come close to admitting that she did have money. Or at least, she would have, one day soon. Then she remembered. She was supposed to be working and not relying on a future living off her inheritance, when it came. Ben reached his hand out and

2

touched her shoulder.

'Look, I do appreciate your enthusiasm and if it were my own place, I wouldn't hesitate. But as you know, it's my mother's pride and joy. I'm just hoping that knowing we're keeping the tea-shop open, will allow her time to make a full recovery.'

Jess pursed her lips. She could understand Ben's difficulty. His mother had suffered a heart attack and in desperation, he had looked for someone to take charge of her beloved tea-shop. He had left his business in London and come to stay in the pretty, little Cornish town of St Withian. He was just about as out of his depth as it was possible to be.

Ben was a businessman through and through, used to dealing with machines rather than people. She smiled. He probably wasn't really so very different from her father, come to think of it.

'Look, I'm very grateful to you. If you hadn't turned up when you did, well, I simply don't know what we'd have done. Mum simply wouldn't let go and was spending every minute of the day worrying herself silly.'

Ben flashed one of his rare smiles. She felt her insides do a strange sort of somersault. Pull yourself together, she ordered herself. What was wrong with her? She wasn't some lovestruck teenager.

Maybe it wasn't just the gorgeous Ben. She was working harder than she had ever worked in her life and actually enjoying it. This particular undertaking was all her own doing. When a distant uncle had died and most unexpectedly left her a large sum of money, she'd had the first of several rows with her parents. Once they'd all got over the shock of why her, she immediately decided to start her own business.

The uncle had made a fortune by starting a business, somewhere in New Zealand and she thought it would be appropriate to follow his lead. But her parents had thought it was a foolish, speculative idea. She didn't have enough experience, or so they said. They wanted her to invest the money in something that would give her a safe income. Not exactly the sort of thing an ambitious twenty-three-year-old would choose. She wanted to have control over her own life, even if she did occasionally make mistakes. She wanted them to be her mistakes.

The trouble with parents was that they never accepted their children could be old enough to manage their own lives. She wasn't planning to use all her money, of course. Jess was enough of her father's daughter to understand the need for some caution. All the same, she needed to have something to do for herself. She gave a small sigh before showing her tempo-rary boss one of her most dazzling smiles.

'Sorry,' she said in her huskiest voice. 'I'm just ambitious, I suppose. I wanted to make some sort of mark on the place. I realise it's probably rather silly. I couldn't expect anyone to spend large sums of money on something so utterly speculative.'

She chose her words carefully, knowing what would make an impact.

Ben nodded his agreement but she could see there had been just a flicker of interest when she mentioned the word speculative. If, as she surmised, he really was something of an entrepreneur, he would take a closer look at her proposals. She turned away and busied herself with tidying up the tables.

The little shop was closed for the day and the woman who came in to wash up and help serve had gone home. Ben was pacing the floor thoughtfully, between casting casual glances over the accounts' books.

'Go through your ideas again,' Ben suggested after a while.

Jess grinned and pulled out the papers she had just stuffed into her capacious handbag and enthusiastically began to explain her ideas.

'If we put a proper roof over the back yard, right up to the end of the building and pushed the kitchen out to there, the existing prep room and kitchen could easily became part of the restaurant, virtually doubling the space available. It wouldn't cost that much at all. We could get over double the covers and even start to add evening meals to the service.

'We could also improve the area outside. Put out tables in the summer and make a sort of patio area. People would kill for a table with that view,' she continued, waving her hands at the expanse of golden sand. 'Then the menu could start to get more interesting than scones and jam. I mean to say, the biggest choice we offer at present is strawberry or raspberry jam.'

She paused for breath.

Ben frowned and pulled out a pen. He began scribbling on the edge of the pages and turned to look round the room. Jess stood anxiously watching, like a child waiting for her teacher to mark her work. She stared at his face watching for any sign of expression that flicked across the handsome features. His dark hair was beginning to take on lighter streaks and the tips of the curls were being gently bleached by the early summer sun. He'd pay a fortune to get the effect in his London hairdresser's. Maybe he did, she thought. He glanced up at her.

'What's up?' he asked, noticing her appraising glance.

She coloured and looked away.

Just appreciating your wonderful looks, her mind was telling her.

'Just wondering what you were thinking,' she managed to say aloud.

His eyes brightened with enthusiasm.

'I was thinking you may just have something here. It's a good plan, well thought out. But my mother would have another heart attack if she had the slightest hint we were thinking of changing as much as a single lace doily. All the same, I'll give it some serious thought. It could just be that my mother won't want to return to work, or indeed be able to work again.'

His mouth tightened momentarily as he faced the worst possibilities.

'Sorry, I mustn't keep you any longer. You'll be wanting to get home.'

Little did he know, she thought. What passed as home here was a dingy room in a block of flats on the edge of the town. The area was deemed too scruffy to let to holidaymakers. Her father would have a fit if he saw the place. He spoke again.

'Unless, that is, you'd like to have a quick drink and talk more about your plans. I've just got time before evening visiting.'

'What? With me?' she burbled.

She was more interested in the man himself than any plans. The thought made her blush. She'd never had such thoughts with most of the men she had met.

'Well, there's no-one else here. Of course I mean you, unless there's some tough, young hunk waiting for you. I don't like violence so I'm afraid I wouldn't be able to fight for your virtue.'

She giggled. She hadn't seen Ben quite so relaxed before.

'I'd love a drink. Thanks.'

Jess checked the back door was locked and everything in the kitchen was turned off. Her father would surely have been impressed at the care she was taking. In his opinion, she was nothing more than an empty-headed child but she desperately wanted to prove him wrong. If only she could get Ben to agree to her ideas, she just knew she would impress her father.

They sat together in the local pub, where the nautical theme of knotted ropes and green glass floats gave a false impression of life by the sea.

'I hope your plans don't include this sort of pseudo-tourist tack,' Ben said wryly.

'Certainly not. White and cool greens with maybe the odd colourful print. We could display work by local artists. There are enough of them around here. It could be a gallery and we can sell for them, at a commission, of course. A few minimal bits and pieces hanging round. Much easier to clean and distinctly more tasteful.'

'I'm glad. Not sure what my mother would think, though. She goes more for the chintz look and copper knick-knacks.'

'Hey, does that mean you are considering my changes?'

He looked at her thoughtfully.

'You haven't told me anything about yourself. Apart from the fact that you can make good scones, brew decent tea and coffee, I have no idea how you came to be in St Withian and be available to work at a moment's notice.'

Jess drew in her breath. Just how much should she tell him? She was very lacking in work references. Probably so lacking, he would never have employed her. But, in his desperation to pacify his mother, he had taken her on, handed her a flower-printed apron and that was it.

Demelza, the waitress, who had refused to take charge herself, was slightly miffed that Ben had brought in a complete stranger. Jess suspected that the woman had been secretly hoping for an unscheduled holiday, on full pay of course. She had been most unco-operative and raised objections wherever she could.

Naturally, Jess had told Ben about her cookery course. She told him she had been cooking and serving high-class meals for large numbers of people for several years. She did not tell him that it had all taken place in the company where her father worked. The business organised conferences and had a consultancy section. It was housed in a large, old country house in Oxford-shire.

Whenever there were visiting clients, Jess had provided lunches and refreshments. It was an understanding rather than an official contract and had paid her just about enough to keep an ancient car on the road and continue living at home. Her mother had great difficulties in moving about, and both parents had been glad to have her help.

She had never had what she would term a proper job. She'd virtually allowed Ben to believe that she'd been running a sort of outside catering business, which in a modest way, wasn't so far from the truth.

'You're very easy to talk to,' she said after a while. 'For a businessman, I mean.'

'Oh, and what exactly is a businessman supposed to sound like? I never realised there was a special breed.'

'Oh, definitely. They only communicate through their secretaries or by electronic mail, have their assistants to do all their 'people things', such as present buying and reminding them when birthdays are imminent.'

'Sounds like you speak from experience. Oh, no,' he went on, having glanced at his watch. 'I'll have to go. Sorry. I'd have liked to chat for longer. Had a meal or something. But, duty calls.'

Jess smiled and said impulsively, 'I

could always come with you to the hospital. Say hello to your mother, reassure her that the business is in good hands. I could slip away and leave you together after a few minutes. Then we could have something to eat in Truro.'

She stopped and realised how dreadfully pushy she must have sounded.

'If you like, I mean. If you've nothing better to do.'

She was blushing hideously, she just knew it. Why could she never control her tongue? The poor man must feel totally trapped.

'Good idea,' he said cheerfully. 'I'm sick of microwave dinners, all alone and far too late after I get back from visiting. Let's go. For heaven's sake, don't breathe a word about any changes.'

She smiled and nodded. In reality, she wanted to hug him, just for taking her seriously. Cancel that thought. She wanted to hug him anyway. For a desk-bound person, he really looked very fit. He must work out, she decided.

Gym? Some sort of rugged sport? There was so much to discover about him. And for once, she was far away from her parents who usually seemed to be looking over her shoulder all the time.

'OK. Here we go,' Ben said as they stopped outside the huge hospital. 'I wanted Mum to go privately but she wouldn't hear of it. Somehow, she can't get used to the idea that I could afford for her to do anything she wants now. She doesn't even need to run her wretched tea-shop but she's so stubborn.'

'I'm looking forward to meeting her.'

'She's a bit formidable. But I don't think you'll find her a problem. Just mind your old-fashioned Ps and Qs and treat her like a piece of fragile bone china.'

Jess lifted an inquiring eyebrow.

'She's always been a bit of duchess, if you know what I mean.'

He smiled at her.

What a smile, she thought, enough to melt inches off any glacier in seconds.

She felt his hand on her elbow, steering her across the crowded carpark.

He glanced at her trim figure and the wonderful dark hair that smelled of something expensive, wondering exactly what his mother would make of her. He hoped she wouldn't start matchmaking again. However attractive Jess might be, he did not want to settle down just yet, especially not if it was at his mother's instigation.

The smart woman with neat, blonde hair was not exactly what Jess had been expecting. Though obviously severely incapacitated by her illness, she was certainly not the frail, little, old lady she had been expecting.

'This is my mother, Margaret Slater. Mum, this is Jessica Davis, the saviour and minor miracle who is keeping your shop going.'

'Tea-rooms, not shop,' Margaret responded, automatically.

She was obviously used to making the distinction.

'How do you do? You look rather too

pretty to be running a proper tea-room. What do you know about home-made baking? Doilies?'

'Hello, Mrs Slater. I hope you're feeling better.'

Jess held out a polite hand to the woman. She could see exactly where Ben had got his extraordinary honey-brown eyes. Those same eyes were currently taking in every minute detail of her looks, her clothes.

'She's an excellent cook, Mum,' Ben said before she could say any more. 'And she places doilies with the most minute care, exactly where they ought to be.'

'And fresh flowers?'

'Of course. Most important for the right atmosphere, I always think.' Jess smiled at her. 'And I've followed your instructions to the letter. Demelza made it very clear how you like things done.'

The woman visibly relaxed and sank into her pillows.

'So you see, Mother, you have nothing to worry about. Submit to everyone's wishes and get yourself fully fit again. Jess can stay as long as you need her. Can't you?'

Again she nodded, thinking for ever wouldn't be too long, provided he was there as well.

'I shall be able to leave her to it and go back to London next week, just to sort out a few things, once I'm sure you're going to be OK, of course.'

He chatted on, encouraging the sick woman not to hurry back to work and suggesting various options for convalescence. Jess scarcely listened, once she heard those dreaded words. Of course he would be going back to his work but suddenly, the whole aspect of the next few weeks had changed. She would be happy to stay on for ever, as long as Ben was going to be around but without him what else was there? A small seaside town, endless scones and the bad-tempered Demelza. Not at all what she'd had in mind. Where was her vision of a smart restaurant with sensational food?

2

'I'll leave you to chat,' Jess said after about half an hour by the hospital bed. 'I'll go down to the coffee bar and give you the chance to talk privately.'

As neither of them protested, she knew she had done the right thing, though she'd have given anything to know what was being said. She picked up a fashion magazine at the counter, an expensive glossy, that she chose at random, and took it to the coffee bar check-out.

She didn't notice when Ben came into the room. He stood behind her and she became aware of the faint scent of him. It was slightly spicy aftershave, nothing too strong but it blended with his natural body scent to give a very potent mix. She turned to him.

'Everything OK?'

They walked out of the café and

towards the main doors.

'She's doing very well. You scored a hit, too. Good job she doesn't realise your intentions for her beloved business or you'd be on your way to the moon at the very least.'

Jess felt relieved. Her new-found sense of independence could never have coped with such instant dismissal.

'So, when do you actually intend returning to the big bad city?' she asked in as light a tone as she could manage.

She was hoping that he might have changed his mind and was planning to stay for much longer.

'Next week sometime. I need to be sure Mother is really on the mend and all is well with you and the shop, sorry, tea-rooms.'

They had reached the carpark and his rather smart car. It quite put Jess's own ancient car into the shade. One of her priorities was to get herself a smart car, once her inheritance came through.

He pressed the remote locking control and continued.

'I'll just need to check on a few things at work. Sort some contracts and stuff and then I'll be back.'

Jess was glad it was dark, so he couldn't see the faint blush of pleasure that ran across her face.

They drove to a small Italian restaurant, tucked away in a side street. Over fresh pasta and a rather good bottle of Chianti, they continued to talk about her ambitious plans. Ben, it seemed, was all in favour. He really liked the idea of something new and different, though, as he acknowledged, there would be many problems to overcome, not the least, convincing his mother.

'Why do you keep staring at me like that?' he asked suddenly.

'I'm sorry. I wasn't aware that I was staring. I'm thinking,' she announced.

'Am I allowed to know the subject of such profound thoughts?'

'You are.' She spoke without thinking. 'I was thinking how lucky it was that I turned up in St Withian that day.'

'Lucky for me, too. The ink was barely dry on the card I was putting up. Why did you drive in to St Withian that day, incidentally?'

'I'd had a row with my parents. They have some notion that I'm letting myself down by not having some flashy job, worthy of my talents, such as they are. But I want to stand on my own two feet, without their help.'

'You strike me as being a very self-assured young woman, quite capable of getting any job and finding your feet. But, you hardly strike me as the sort of woman who'd be content with managing a small restaurant.'

She pursed her lips. He was right. She wanted to run it with complete autonomy, not simply manage the place for some elderly lady limited to jam and scones. She intended to make it a major outlet with an excellent reputation. He continued.

'The way you speak for a start. Your accent suggests you had a good education.'

'Are we to have a pudding?' she asked, steering the subject away from the dangerous ground of her past and her limited experience of work.

'How can you stay so slim after eating a huge plate of pasta and still want some calorie-laden pudding?'

'I take it that was a no. Oh, well. Can't win 'em all, as they say. At least allow me some coffee.'

He laughed.

'Have whatever you like. You obviously have a good appetite. Makes a refreshing change after some of the women I know. If food has the slightest calorie above their daily target, it's a no-no. You know, I think I'll even join you in something wickedly chocolate-laden.'

As they ate, she probed for more information about him as a person, but he seemed as unwilling to talk about himself as she was. She managed to discover that he owned a company that produced computer software and that he was very successful. He had set up the tea-room for his mother after his father had died, to provide her with an occupation.

It had rarely broken even but he helped in subtle ways, managing the books himself and hiding the fact that things were not as good as she thought. He'd recognised at once how important it was for her to have an interest.

Jess tried to steer him towards talk about his private life but he would not be drawn. He must surely have some sort of relationship, she tried to tell herself. He was undoubtedly quite a catch, rich, good-looking . . . the sort of man any woman would find attractive. She saw that he was looking at her intently and had she but realised it, his thoughts were echoing her own.

He was wondering if she had a relationship with anyone. More importantly, he was asking himself what she was doing in Cornwall, working in a tiny tea-room. None of it made much sense to him. She had the sort of confidence that came from a

24

professional training or a background of some independence. But her words belied these thoughts.

They drove back to St Withian and as he stopped outside the tea-shop, Ben leaned over and kissed her lightly on top of her hair. It was an unexpected gesture which delighted her. Momentarily breathless, she couldn't speak. Where had her usual confidence gone?

'I've enjoyed this evening,' he said softly. 'And again, thank you so much for holding the fort this way. I'll certainly give some thought to your suggestions but don't hold your breath. I'm really not sure what my mother intends to do, long-term. Maybe she will still need to hang on to the business, if only to give her the motivation to get better.'

'Yes,' she said. 'You're probably right. It's unfair to even think of changing things.'

'Are you sure I can't drop you off at your home? I don't even know where you live.'

She felt ashamed of the grotty, little flat and wished she had somewhere smart to invite him back for coffee.

'I'm fine. But thanks anyway. I have my car parked round the back.'

'We must do this again sometime, if you'd like to, of course.'

She nodded, knowing her cheeks were a fiery red in the darkness.

'Mm, I'd love to. Thank you. And thanks again for this evening. I've really enjoyed myself.'

She climbed out of his car and with a casual wave, walked through the arch that led to the back of the tea-room. Her emotions felt ridiculously jangled. It wasn't as if she hadn't had boyfriends before. There had been several but never anyone who'd lasted for long.

Her father, in particular, had taken the 'only daughter' thing much too far. No-one was ever good enough for her. Left to his requirements for a boy-friend, Jess would be lucky to find anyone before she was ninety.

Impulsively, she took out her mobile,

her parent's gift last birthday. He'd insisted on knowing she could always contact them. She dialled her home, feeling somewhat guilty about leaving her mother in the lurch. It wasn't that she didn't care but both she and her mother knew she should be trying to achieve more in her life.

As the number was ringing, she thought again about her distant uncle and the amazing windfall that he had left her. It was like a dream — money from a relation you didn't know at all and would, therefore, not really miss. He'd evidently had no family of his own and selected her as his beneficiary, almost at random, it seemed.

There was no reply from home and she hoped everything was all right. The answering machine cut in but she didn't want to leave a message. When her inheritance finally arrived, she fully intended spending a large chunk on getting someone to help her mother. Though they had a cleaner once a week, Jess wanted someone to be more of a companion to her mother, someone able to help in the tasks her mother was no longer able to accomplish herself.

Her thoughts returned to Ben as she drove home. Her father's belief was that when a man knew Jess was rich, she would be a target for every get-rich-quick merchant in town. Not exactly flattering, Jess had told him. In her heart, she already knew that Ben was different.

She also knew that she felt differently about him than she had ever felt about anyone before.

It was ridiculous, considering she knew almost nothing about him and had only met him a few days ago. There was something very special about him and it was endearing that he so obviously cared so much for his mother. As she reached her awful flat, she also realised how much she loved and missed her parents. She would call them again as soon as she was home. She spoke into her mobile this time, and left her message.

'Mum? Dad? I'm sorry I flounced off like that. I know you were only trying to look after me, just as you always have. But I'm a big girl now and you should know that I'll always look after myself. I love you both. I'm actually working very hard and really enjoying myself. I'll call again soon, promise. 'Bye.'

She felt tears in her eyes as she spoke. Homesickness, she assumed. It wasn't exactly the home she missed, more her parents and their loving ways. Perhaps that was all that homesickness meant. Snap out of it, she instructed herself.

Jess glanced round the rather unpleasant room. If Ben agreed to go ahead with the restaurant idea, she would get herself somewhere decent to live. This place was a purely temporary measure, just to go with her purely temporary job.

Early the next day, she arrived at the tea-shop and began to make the morning quota of scones. She was efficient and soon the aroma of baking filled the shop. She began to lift down the chairs from the tables but stopped, knowing it would infuriate the difficult Demelza. She hated any of her jobs to be touched and this was her morning chore.

Jess decided to be rash and make some different things to sell with the morning coffees. There was a poor selection of ingredients but enough to put together a couple of gateaux and some tasty cookies. She could pop to the health shop once Demelza arrived and buy a few extras to add flavour to her new lines.

Predictably, the woman was highly critical of the changes to the menu. She removed her scarf and coat, her personal uniform, winter and summer alike.

'People round here don't like change. They like things done the way they always are,' she sniffed.

'I hope you're not starting a cold,' Jess asked solicitously, following the whole barrage of disapproving sniffs.

'Don't know what you're talking about,' the reply came.

'I'm just going to the health-food shop. Few things I need,' Jess announced as she went out of the door.

Demelza glared. Orders were written out on Mondays and delivered Tuesdays. There was no call for extra things to be bought. Fancy ideas, all rubbish. People only ever wanted the scones, jam and cream. Whatever Mrs Slater would say, she hated to think.

A small table in the window was used to display the scones, covered with old-fashioned glass domes as a gesture towards complying with hygiene rules. Today, two of the domes covered Jess's gateaux and healthy-looking cookies. Several new people stopped to look and some of them came into the shop, much to Demelza's annoyance. She tried to palm them off with their usual food but within the first half hour, they were sold out.

Jess was delighted. Maybe the town

wasn't quite so negative about something new after all.

The next day, she expanded the menu again, this time adding several types of quiche to serve at lunchtime. Demelza was positively furious.

'I'm not paid to do lunches,' she grumbled. 'We normally sits down and has a cuppa ourselves, not get rushed off our feet like this.'

'I didn't know you were starting lunch menus,' one of the town's elderly ladies announced. 'I shall suggest our little group might meet here once a fortnight, if you can provide something suitable.'

'You'll have to talk to the temporary manager,' the sulky waitress snapped. 'She's only here while Mrs Slater gets over her illness.'

'Ask her to come out from the kitchen, will you, dear?' the customer said.

Sulkily, Demelza went into the kitchen. Jess was flushed from the heat of oven and also from the fact that she'd spotted Ben's car stopping in the little yard at the back.

'Someone wants you,' Demelza snapped. 'About the food.'

'What's wrong with the food?' Ben asked anxiously, as he came into the kitchen.

'How should I know? I'm only the waitress. Some woman asked to see the cook.'

She swung out again as Jess looked at Ben. If only he didn't make her heart miss a beat, she would have been able to answer coherently.

'Shall I deal with it?' he offered.

'Of course not. If someone has a complaint, I'll deal with it.'

She straightened her apron and rammed the obligatory catering hat farther on to her head and went into the shop. The woman was looking out for her and signalled, as Jess crossed to the table.

'Is something wrong?' she asked, putting on her best smile.

'Wrong? Of course not. In fact just

the opposite. Are you responsible for this delicious quiche?'

Jess nodded, relief flooding through her.

'If you can produce meals like this, then I'd like to make a booking for our ladies'-group lunch next week. We meet on Wednesdays, once a fortnight. We have been looking for somewhere new, to provide simple, tasty food. Somewhere with a nice atmosphere, you understand. We often call here for coffee but I didn't realise you were planning an expansion. Can you manage it? Twelve of us, next Wednesday.'

Jess blushed with pleasure.

'Of course, we can. I will just need to check our bookings though. But I'm sure next Wednesday is free. We are only doing simple cold lunches at present, quiche and salad. And I can do something like profiteroles for a pudding, or gateaux, of course.'

'Excellent. I'm Mrs Minty, by the way.'

She handed Jess a card with her telephone number.

'Call me if there's a problem. Otherwise, we'll see you at twelve-thirty next Wednesday.'

She paid her bill, mollified Demelza with a larger than usual tip and swept out. Jess went back to the kitchen, punching the air with a hissed, 'Yes,' escaping from her lips.

'Well, well,' Ben said as she grinned up at him. 'So, we've already added lunches to our services, have we?'

Her smile faded. He looked annoyed, she realised.

'I'm sorry. I should have asked you first, only when I thought Demelza had received a complaint I was relieved, and, well, I just went ahead without thinking.'

'You really have got the bit between your teeth, haven't you? Look, I don't mind but don't overstretch yourself, or the business. I understand you wanting to expand but we might not be able to keep up with it, not for long.'

'You can bet your life we won't. What on earth would Mrs Slater say? Does she know what's going on?' Demelza said as she dumped a pile of dirty plates on the clean counter. 'I'm not paid for this sort of thing.'

There was a glint in her eye that gave Jess a momentary concern.

'It's only a few light lunches,' Jess protested.

'Yes, and where's it all going to lead? That's what I'd like to know. You'll expect me to wear myself out serving them all. Washing up as well. I'm not willing to wash great piles of cutlery and sticky pots.'

'We are considering getting a dishwasher,' Ben said unexpectedly.

'Are we?' Jess said in surprise. 'Yes, of course we are,' she corrected hurriedly.

'Don't hold with them things, all electricity and water. Not safe. Shouldn't mix electric and wet stuff.'

Demelza left with another sniff.

'Don't know what the boss will say,' she muttered as she was going.

'I couldn't think of anyone less like Demelza, if I tried,' Jess said.

They both burst out laughing.

'And what's with this dishwasher idea?'

'I was thinking we'd get a small, industrial one. I'll check out some prices. I thought we could have one standing on the side next to the sink. What do you think?'

Jess nodded happily. Wherever they went from here, they would need a dishwasher and even if nothing further happened, it would certainly make life easier for Margaret when and if she returned to the business.

'I hope you didn't really mind my trying a few new ideas. I made some gateaux yesterday, as you probably gathered. They sold really well and that's why I did the quiches today. I know your mother may not want the extra work, but I can easily cope while I'm here. I was sure I'd still be here at least next week and so the lunch booking seemed reasonable.'

He reassured her and said he was pleased she had shown such initiative. He was looking round the kitchen while they talked, almost as if he was assessing the potential. She made no comment, knowing it was wiser to leave him to think for a while.

'Look, I have to go back to London for a couple of days. I'll organise the dishwasher from a dealer I know. He'll advise on the right one to get. I'll call you. I shall only be away for a couple of days. Don't do anything else too rash, will you? No wholesale contracts with local suppliers just yet. We need to explore the market a bit more. Visit some of the other places in the area.'

'Sounds like it could be fun,' she said wistfully.

The prospect of a few evenings out with Ben, visiting the potential rivals to a restaurant sounded promising.

'Right, well, I'll be on my way. My mother is aware that I won't be visiting for a couple of days and, hopefully, there won't be any problems here. Are you all right for cash, for orders and things?'

'Sure.' She nodded. 'There will just be Demelza's wages and I expect there will be enough in the till for that. I can have mine when you get back. No problems.'

He stood by the door, slightly uncertainly, as if he was wondering how to say goodbye. Jess smiled at him and turned back to the sink, slightly dismissively.

She felt herself longing to throw herself into his arms and wish him a safe journey but it seemed all wrong here. She caught a movement out of the corner of her eye and saw Demelza turn back into the shop.

Now what would she have made of Jess's thoughts? She wondered what the woman had overheard of their earlier conversation and hoped that if she did hear anything, she wouldn't pass on the information to Mrs Slater.

3

Just two days after Ben had left St Withian, an engineer arrived with a dishwasher. Naturally, Demelza refused to use it and complained bitterly the entire morning. Jess gave up trying to persuade her that it was all for the best and simply put the dirty dishes in the machine herself.

It certainly made a difference, with sparkling clean cups and saucers coming out in no time at all.

Ben had certainly proved his efficiency. What a pity he had not yet returned to brighten the rest of her day. When she closed at five-thirty, Demelza seemed in rather a rush to leave. She obviously had some mission, some plan for the evening.

Jess was to suffer the consequences the next morning, when she received an anxious phone call from the hospital. It seemed the waitress had done her worst when she had visited Margaret Slater in hospital the previous evening.

'Jessica?' Margaret's slightly strident voice asked. 'I understand from Demelza that you are making a vast number of changes to my business. I am not at all pleased. How could you, when you know I specifically asked that nothing should be altered?'

As soon as she paused for breath, Jess was able to speak.

'I've only put on the odd few extra dishes, just while I'm here. Nothing elaborate,' she said, crossing her fingers at the slight fib.

'But I gather you've ordered some new machinery, taking up valuable space.'

'Ben got us a dishwasher. It's brilliant. So much more hygienic and faster than any of us could be.'

'Ben arranged it? You're quite sure you didn't order it yourself?'

'Of course not. As if I'd do such a thing. But it will make things much easier for you. That was really why he bought it. I believe it was to be his gift to you, to make things easier for you when you return. It's very efficient.'

Jess hoped she was saying the right things.

'But what's this about providing lunches? I can't do lunches. I haven't the time or energy.'

'Please, Mrs Slater, don't worry. You mustn't give it a thought until you are quite better. It was really a favour to Mrs Minty.'

She caught sight of the woman's card by the telephone and realised that she must be known to Mrs Slater.

'Anything I do can be stopped as soon as you return, if you don't want to continue with it. I'm so sorry you were bothered with any of this.'

'Yes, well. Understandably, Demelza was quite concerned and thought I should know.'

The poor lady sounded edgy and slightly breathless.

For five more minutes, Jess reassured

Ben's mother that all was well. She did feel slightly guilty about it, in view of her other plans for the business but she said nothing to upset Mrs Slater. She would certainly have words with the waitress later, she promised herself. Demelza had no right to go and upset a sick woman that way. All the same, Jess couldn't afford for her to walk out, however unsatisfactory she might be. There was no way she could manage the place alone.

The atmosphere was distinctly chilly throughout the day. It was during the lull between lunch and afternoon teas when Ben walked into the kitchen. Jess felt a tingle of pleasure when he arrived but her smile soon faded when she saw his expression.

'What on earth have you been saying to my mother?' he demanded. 'I specifically told you not to upset her. If you think you'd steal a march by trying to persuade her, you were wrong. You can forget all your plans. You've done yourself no favours by trying to go behind my back.'

'Excuse me. May I ask what you're talking about? I haven't even seen your mother. I did speak to her first thing this morning and tried my best to reassure her that I hadn't been ruining her business.'

'Then however did she find out about your little schemes in the first place?'

'I gathered that Demelza went to visit her last night.'

'Demelza? You mean she told Mum? How much did she know?'

'I suppose she must have overheard us talking. Your mother is all right, isn't she?'

'Not really. No. She's had a relapse. The hospital called to tell me this morning and, of course, I rushed back immediately. Managed to get a flight from Gatwick and then had to hire a car. But the doctor said she must not be stressed in any way. Damn it, this is the last thing I needed. Maybe I'd better see Demelza and sort things out. I won't have it. Rank interference.'

'I still don't think you should sack her. Your mother will need her when she gets back home. I'm so sorry, Ben. I really thought I'd calmed her down. I even told her the dishwasher was your gift to help her when she returned to work.'

'She even knew about the dishwasher? I bet that went down well. I've tried to persuade her to bring one in for years. She rather shared Demelza's views.'

Ben calmed down and, tight-lipped, he went into the tea-room. Jess watched carefully from the back but she could hear nothing. Demelza's face crumpled slightly and she watched Ben's anger drain slowly. She hoped she would never have to face his anger. He stormed out, as quickly as he had arrived and calmly, Jess began to organise the teas as customers drifted in.

At the end of the day, Demelza left and wearily, Jess wiped down the counters. Her heart pounded as she saw

Ben's hired car stop outside. Was she about to get the sack? He came in and flopped down at one of the tables.

'You look all in. Shall I make you some tea?'

He nodded, propping his head on his hands.

'My mother's in quite a state. What on earth possessed that woman to go and upset her like that. It's beyond me.'

'I expect she was looking after herself. I'm sorry about your mother. Will she get better?'

'I hope so. But I somehow doubt she will be coming back here. I have to decide what to do.'

'You could always let me buy you out,' Jess said suddenly.

'You?' Ben scoffed. 'Where would you get that sort of money? It may not look much but property prices here are rocketing.'

Jess bit her lip. The words had come out in her usual careless way. She could understand his surprise.

'Just call it momentary madness,' she

said flippantly, hoping he might laugh.

'The way I feel at present, if I thought you may be serious, I'd jump at the chance. I suppose you're not some rich heiress, are you?'

He laughed as she blushed slightly and looked away.

'I thought not. Never mind. As if anyone with serious money would want this rundown little dump.'

'Better not let your mother hear you talking like that.'

'Sorry. I'm tired and depressed. Have you eaten yet? No, of course you haven't. Could you bear to keep a misery like me company?' he asked.

'I'd love to. I'll even allow you to tell me all your problems.'

'You don't want to know. I fancy a large meal and too much wine. What do you say?'

'Maybe I should drive,' she suggested and he smiled and nodded.

'We'll go somewhere very expensive and drown our sorrows.'

'I should go home and change first. I

could do with a shower after cooking all day. Could I meet you somewhere?'

She wanted to avoid taking him to her awful flat but no way would she go somewhere special, looking like this. Finally, he insisted on meeting her at the end of the road and she had to agree.

She drove her ancient car back to her flat and changed into the one decent outfit she'd crammed into her suitcase when she'd left her home. She brushed her damp hair and left the curls hanging loose. She grabbed a woolly stole to put round her bare shoulders and stepped outside the flat. It was a beautiful evening but slightly chilly.

She went to the corner of the road to wait for Ben. A taxi stopped and she was about to wave it on, when Ben opened the rear door.

'I thought we'd both be able to enjoy a drink if we didn't have to drive,' he explained.

'Thank you. That was thoughtful,' she said as she got in beside him.

'Selfish more like. I phoned the hospital by the way, and Mum's resting comfortably. They preferred I didn't visit again anyhow, so we're free to enjoy the evening. I thought we'd visit a place a little way along the coast. If we did ever go ahead with refurbishing the café, sorry tea-room,' he corrected with a grin, 'I'd like to think we might be able to aim for something like this place. It's primarily a fish restaurant, with locally caught fish, of course.'

'I'd like to use all local produce, vegetables, meat, everything. We could also do a range of special vegetarian dishes, go organic maybe. The demand is growing.'

Jess's enthusiasm was also growing by the minute, as she talked of ideas as they occurred to her. It was exciting to be able to talk to a relative stranger about things she'd only dreamed of before.

Several times, she almost told him of the legacy she was about to receive but she kept herself in check. If her father was remotely correct about her being befriended simply for her money, she wanted to be able to prove something, especially with Ben. It was ridiculous, she knew, but her pride made the decision for her.

'I like a lot of what you are saying,' Ben concluded over coffee. 'You're imaginative and though I think some of it may be over-ambitious, I do believe it could work. Persuading my mother is the biggest hurdle we'd have to cross.'

'What about the money?' she said hesitantly. 'I know I said it wouldn't cost all that much, but in truth, it will cost a tidy sum. We'd have all sorts of expenses to launch into the market we'd need to target.'

'I suppose if Mother approved, she would turn the business over to me, eventually. I couldn't risk too many of my assets into this. My main business would suffer.'

'What if I were able to provide, say, half the capital? Would you consider a partnership?'

'You would do that? Take out a loan on something so speculative?'

'Don't concern yourself with the hows. I would be willing to take a half share.'

'But you'd also be doing most of the work. I'd really only be a sleeping partner.'

Jess laughed at his words and a grin broke over his own handsome face as he realised the full meaning of the words he'd used. He reached across the table and took her hand lightly.

'You're a lovely woman,' he said, suddenly serious. 'Just the sort of woman my mother would be trying to match me with. But I doubt she'd approve of you one jot, if she knew what you were really after.'

'And what do you think I may be after, as you put it?'

'The business, of course. What else?'

He then coloured slightly as once more he saw a deeper meaning in his words. Jess bit her lip once more. She was allowing her mouth to run away with her once again. Poor Ben. He looked so uncomfortable for a moment. She disengaged her hand from his and folded her napkin, desperately trying to change the subject.

'That was a lovely meal. Thank you so much.'

'Thank you for listening so patiently to my moans.'

'You haven't moaned at all. Honestly,' she assured him.

He went to pay the bill and she picked up her bag, standing back a short way as he settled the bill. He looked thoughtful as he glanced at the figures.

'What do you think that cost?' he said slightly impolitely.

'I don't have a clue. There were no prices on my menu.'

'Really?'

He looked surprised.

'It's supposed to be a ploy to prevent guests from being embarrassed by the cost of the various dishes. So you don't feel you have to choose the cheapest things.'

'Good gracious. I never knew that,' he said. 'Well, well.'

'It's very common in most cities. I'm surprised you've never discovered it in London.'

'I'm usually doing business meals. I rarely eat out purely socially. Anyhow, what do you think that might have cost per head, if I say it's a high class, expensive place?'

He was smiling as he spoke. Jess frowned and then decided she was as likely to make an accurate guess as try to work it out. She named a figure at random. He nodded, his lips paused.

'And does that include drinks?' he asked.

Jess pulled a face. It must have been extortion if he had to ask that.

'Was I so far out?' she asked, as they got into their taxi.

'I'd be interested to know what you would have charged for a meal like that in our restaurant.'

'Our restaurant? I like the sound of

that. I'd need to think a bit about it. I can work out the cost of ingredients easily enough and add the margins but not in my head. And certainly not after all that wine and with the pre-dinner drinks as well.'

'OK, I was being unfair. You were just about right, as a matter of fact. I thought it was a bit steep, but then, I don't know very much about it anyhow. Now, where shall we drop you?'

Jess opted for the end of the road again, still sensitive about her accommodation.

'Thank you again. I really enjoyed the evening.'

As she climbed the stairs to her flat, she contemplated the future. What would her parents think if she moved down here to Cornwall on a permanent basis? Did she really want to make her home down here? Was it simply Ben who was the attraction? A very difficult decision would have to be made.

★ ★ ★

Ben was in and out of the tea-rooms for several days. He spent a great deal of time at the hospital where his mother was, at last, beginning to recover. Jess worked very hard, doing half of Demelza's chores as well as managing the cooking. She resorted to bags of pre-washed salads from the local supermarket, calling in on her way to work.

The morning coffees and cream teas were still popular but there was a growing clientèle for the simple lunches she was providing. The apparently weary waitress complained non-stop as Jess managed the dishwasher, cooking and laying trays for her to take out. On more than one occasion, Jess was tempted to tell her to pack up her things and go but remembering that it wasn't her place, she ignored the constant barbed comments. When they finally managed a short break, Jess sank into a chair.

'I'm shattered,' she announced. 'Can you make me one of the herbal teas?'

'Don't know how. Fancy rubbish.'

Demelza was predictably hostile.

'Never mind,' Jess said wearily. 'Ordinary tea will do.'

Demelza went into the kitchen, grumbling as she went.

'Thinks I'm some sort of servant. Cheeky madam.'

Jess bit back the words. How many cups of tea and coffee and scones had she prepared for the woman? She came back and dumped a cup on the table, spilling the contents into the saucer.

'All right if I go now? I want to get the bus to Truro and see the boss this evening.'

'I think Ben would prefer it if you didn't visit his mother. You upset her badly the last time you went.'

'It's my duty to tell her what's going on here. She asked me to keep her informed,' Demelza snapped.

'You must telephone Ben first,' Jess insisted. 'He said you should not visit her again, not without his permission.'

'I don't know how you've got the

bare-faced cheek to tell me what I can and can't do,' she continued. 'I've known Mrs Slater for ten years or more. She's a real lady and knows how things should be done. I'm going to see her, whether you like it or not. Think you can come in here and take over. And don't think you've got any chance with that Ben. Mrs Slater has him just where she wants him. Besides, he's virtually engaged. Be married by the end of the year, I don't doubt. Now then, I think I may have one of my headaches coming on. I may not be in tomorrow.'

She grabbed her coat and scarf, slamming the door as she stormed out.

'Don't you dare let me down tomorrow,' Jess hissed after the retreating figure. 'Mrs Minty and her crew are coming for lunch.'

Suddenly drained of all energy, Jess put her head down on the table and began to sob. If the wretched Demelza was going to let her down, she needed to get well ahead with the cooking tonight. And she ought to let Ben know what the woman intended doing at the hospital. She picked up the phone and dialled his mobile number, leaving a message when he failed to answer.

She then went into the kitchen and began grating cheese.

'Three quiches and there's still the profiteroles to make,' she muttered. 'I may get home for midnight, if I'm lucky.'

4

By the time Jess collapsed into her bed, it was indeed, almost midnight. She'd worked hard all evening, trying to ensure that everything was perfect for the next day. Besides, the work had gone some way to stave off the disappointment of discovering that Ben had some sort of relationship. She never doubted Demelza's words for a moment. She felt more disappointed than she could say.

She set the alarm for seven the next morning, knowing she'd never wake up in time without it. It still seemed like the middle of the night when she took her shower and set off for work. She set to work in the kitchen, collecting her serving dishes and putting plates to one side.

Nine o'clock arrived but Demelza didn't. Quickly, Jess took down the chairs and arranged the tables. In less than half an hour, the first morning coffee customers would be arriving and she still had masses to do for lunch.

'Don't do this to me, Demelza,' she snarled through bared teeth.

But the woman was doing it and she knew there had been every intention to let her down from the first moment they had spoken of the lunches. It was pay-back time for the disruption to the woman's comfortable little life. Thank heavens she had worked long and late the previous evening.

She set the electric boiler to heat and took out the trays of scones from the oven. The extra items she'd been adding to the menu would have to be minimal today, she thought. Like a whirlwind, she dashed round the kitchen, trying to cover the necessary chores before customers were demanding her attention. She heard the shop bell ring and sighed.

'Here we go,' she muttered as she fixed her smile and went to greet the two ladies who were deciding which table would be the best for them.

For over an hour she brewed pot after pot of coffee and served numerous plates of scones, jam and cream. The one gateau she had managed to make had disappeared within half an hour. She flung dirty dishes into the machine, organised salads and was almost frantic by eleven-thirty, with all her efforts. The till was becoming reassuringly full and, in part, made up for some of the hassle, but the time for the luncheon group's arrival was pressing.

She was trying to move tables around and set them up when more customers arrived for coffee. She swore under her breath at Demelza's untimely absence and smiled a welcome to the new-comers.

'Oh, I didn't realise you took lunch bookings,' one of them said as they saw the reserved sign she had hastily contrived. 'Can you fit in four more today?'

Jess took a breath and before she

could say anything, a voice behind her chipped in.

'Of course, madam. Simple lunches, you understand. As we have a larger booking today, we can't offer more than the set menu.'

Jess stared, her admiration mixed with irritation as Ben was speaking.

'If you can give us half an hour, we shall be ready to begin our lunch service. Perhaps you'd like some coffee to be going on with?'

The four women nodded and sat down at a table. Ben went into the kitchen and looked helplessly at the coffee pots and the electric boiler.

'What on earth do I have to do?' he moaned.

Jess laughed.

'Welcome aboard. I'll set up the tray and you can be waiter.'

Efficiently, she put cups and saucers on the tray and added all the necessary accoutrements. She turned back to the oven and put the quiches to warm. To save time, she wrapped the cutlery in napkins thinking that as Ben was here, he could at least put them out on the tables. His timely arrival was exactly what she needed to get the lunches organised.

'So, where's the fair Demelza?' he demanded.

'Dunno,' Jess replied as she juggled pans on the tiny cooker top. 'She threatened she might be getting one of her headaches yesterday. It must have actually happened.'

'Like heck. She wanted you to come a cropper over the lunch thing. I bet there's nothing wrong with her.'

'Who knows? How's your mother, by the way?'

'Coming on. I just hope nothing sets her back again. Now, these ready to go out?'

He picked up the cutlery and a tray of glasses and went into the main room.

By two-fifteen, they were busily rearranging the room again for the afternoon tea trade. Jess felt as if she never wanted to see food again but all the same, she felt a glow of pleasure at the thought of the many nice comments she had received. The ladies wanted to re-book for their following meeting. She hesitated, wondering if she would still be there in two weeks but Ben was very positive and immediately wrote it on the calendar.

She took out yet another tray of scones from the oven and began to make up some dishes of jam. Without Demelza, today had been a nightmare. Without Ben it would have been a total disaster.

'I reckon this is probably the best day this café has ever seen, as far as takings go. This town obviously needs somewhere like this. Well done,' he said as he stuffed a load of notes into an envelope and put it in his pocket. 'When I pay that lot in, Mother's overdraft will be looking much healthier.'

'I'm glad. But I have actually paid for a lot of the stuff myself, with cash. There didn't seem to be anything arranged for ingredients, apart from the cream and some basics.'

Ben looked horrified and immediately took out the envelope again.

'It's OK. I have all the bills. We'll sort it out later,' Jess said.

'If you're sure. Can you manage now? Only I really have to get back to other things.'

'Of course. I'm sorry you were bothered but, well, I could never have predicted Demelza's actions, could I?'

'Maybe not. She's . . . well, I'll just say, unreliable, in the circumstances. We can't dismiss her though, as Mum is very fond of her. They built the place up together. She trusts her, too.'

'Fine. Well, being charitable, maybe she really was ill. Give my regards to your mother and assure her, all is going well.'

'If I eventually get around to seeing her, I will. I have other things to think about at the moment, though.'

He left her and she wondered what else was on his mind. Clearly, something was. She shrugged. He hadn't expected to become a waiter when he'd arrived so perhaps he was simply tired after the unaccustomed work. Then he heard the shop bell ring and went to serve the latest customers.

Jess spent a quiet evening alone in her poky little flat, feeling totally exhausted. She tried to make some notes for her new ideas and opened a few books to sort out some recipes but all the time, Ben's face intruded on her thoughts. Though the first seeds of her idea for 'something in catering' were beginning to grow, the thought of spending her time in someone else's café — tea-room, as Margaret insisted — wasn't quite what she'd had in mind.

Under the circumstances, though, it was proving an excellent start. Ben was undoubtedly the big draw but she knew so little about him. They'd shared a couple of meals at a time when he was feeling down in the dumps over his mother's illness but she had only a very small part of the picture. She knew he was unmarried but did she really have any idea of his private life? He may well have a girlfriend, as Demelza was hinting, whether his mother knew it or not. But Ben or no Ben, was her own future really in Cornwall? Did she want to be here or not?

It was a big decision to make after so short a time. She realised that the tea-room was so exactly what she had been thinking about, even if it did need radical changes to make it become all that she was hoping for. She sighed, knowing she was accomplishing nothing. She had to admit, Cornwall was very attractive but if Ben didn't come as part of the deal, was she still willing to be part of it? She spoke out loud, as if it would clarify her thoughts.

'You're a silly woman. You're acting as though you're in love with a man that you hardly know. You're a grown woman and it's time you started behaving like one.'

Thoroughly self-chastised, she put the kettle on to make a drink. She needed an early night and certainly didn't need to sit mooning about a man who was clearly out of her reach.

★   ★   ★

At eighty-thirty next morning, Jess was already clearing the chairs from the tables after sweeping the floor. She put out the flowers and nodded with her approval at the sight of the tidy room.

If Demelza deigned to put in an appearance, then she'd have even less work to do and so couldn't complain. She went into the kitchen to start on the daily batch of cooking. To her surprise, Ben knocked on the rear door, smiling through the window.

'What are you doing here so early?' she asked.

'Thought I'd better come and see if your helper has turned up today. I didn't want you so over-worked that you left us in desperation.'

'No sign so far but it is only nine o'clock. She often gets here rather later than this.'

'If she wasn't close to my mother, I'd tell her where to go. I think she's really been taking advantage over the years. Maybe we should get someone else in. Part-time.'

'Can we afford it? I mean, if we don't sack Demelza, we'll have two lots of wages to pay.'

'Leave it to me. I'll sort something. Meanwhile, put a card on the door. Someone might see it and apply right away. Put **Temporary Position** and that way we're not committed to anything long term. Now, if you're OK for the time being, I'll drive round to Demelza's home and see what's going on.'

He put a comforting hand on her arm and strode out.

Jess smiled to herself as she watched him. He was so confident and sure of himself. Tactful, too, no doubt. No wonder his mother adored him. Wouldn't any female? Those charms were about to be used on the wretched Demelza. What effect might they have on her? She supposed that somehow, the woman would have to accept that her position was slightly less secure than it always had been.

Quarter-of-an-hour later, the woman herself appeared, carrying a large bag full of supplies.

'Good morning,' Jess said politely. 'I hope you're feeling better today.'

''Morning. I'm feeling awful, if you must know, but I didn't want to let Mrs Slater down. I turned in anyway. I collected the cream and extra things as I always do on Thursdays.'

'Oh, I just ordered a new batch to be delivered.'

Jess felt irritated.

'I didn't see that everything had to be changed during your temporary stay here. Mrs Slater will want things properly back to normal when she comes back. I see you've done the tables. I suppose you thought I wouldn't come in today. Well, you don't know me, do you? I don't let people down.'

She went to the back and put on her overall and began to rub at the already spotless tables and re-adjust the flowers.

'We need more flowers. I'll go and get them later.'

'I think those will do for today. Perhaps you can sort out the cutlery trays. They are in a bit of a muddle after the hectic day I had yesterday. Ben himself came to help me out.'

'Poor man. He doesn't want to be bothered with such things. I hope he wasn't forced to tell his mother how you're using him.'

She turned away muttering something about pretty faces and thinking people could get what they wanted from a man daft enough to fall for it. Jess went back into the kitchen and began her chores.

A few moments later the back door opened and Ben came in.

'The wretched woman wasn't home. I don't know where she's got to.'

Jess made a warning signal and

pointed through to the main room.

'Oh, Mr Ben. I'm so sorry to have let you down yesterday. If I'd once thought she'd call you in, I'd have struggled in somehow. I'm so sorry. I'm not well today but I know my duty to your poor mother. How is she, by the way?'

Her simpering tone made Jess feel slightly sick but her face remained a mask of indifference.

'She's OK. Holding her own. But we're not out of the wood yet. It's going to take a long time.'

'You mean she's going to be here for an indefinite time?' she snapped, jerking her thumb towards Jess. 'I just hope your poor mother's got a business left at the end of it. All these changes. Mrs Slater'll never be able to cope with all the changes she's making.'

'Perhaps you'd like to step into the other room,' Ben said tactfully.

Jess continued her work without comment. She lined up the day's baking on cooling racks and continued her routine. She could hear subdued voices from the shop area but could hear nothing of the actual words. She felt entirely confident that Ben would take her side and waited to see what was going to happen. At last, he came into the kitchen.

'We've agreed that Demelza should have some extra help,' he said blandly. 'I'm going to put up a card right away and we'll try to get someone to help with the lunches. She can't manage to wait at table and do the washing up, even with the machine.'

'But I organise all the washing up,' Jess burst out, unable to stop herself. 'And I do all the cooking and set up the trays. She only has to carry them to the tables.'

'And deal with all the complicated bills,' Demelza protested as she joined them in the kitchen. 'And take the money and check the till. It's too much these days, since you made it all so difficult. Before it was always the same. Same price for everything and no extra messy gateaux and all. Now, if you'll excuse me, I have to go out and buy fresh flowers. Mrs Slater'd have a fit if she saw those pathetic dead daisies. At least I can make sure standards are kept in some aspects of her lovely little tea-rooms.'

Jess glared at Ben, waiting for him to say something. He smiled, melting her very bones with his slow, dark look. She felt herself feeling weak and wished she was still able to make the sparky retort that was waiting inside her brain.

'Hey, come on. You can easily get your new waitress on your side and she can ease your pressure. Remember my mother. She'd have further problems if she thought we'd sacked Demelza. I'm not willing to risk it. Oh, I've left some cash for her on the desk. She'd paid for ingredients apparently. Does it every week or so she says.'

'So I gather. If I'd known, I'd never have ordered everything to be delivered. I've set up a temporary account with a small wholesaler. Hope that's OK. Still, I suppose we'll get through all the ingredients soon enough.'

'Maybe we should continue our research into local eating places. You free tonight? I'll try to get to the hospital early and pick you up around eight.'

'That would be great,' she said happily.

Whatever Demelza had said to warn her off, she wasn't about to turn down an evening with Ben. As she watched him leave, she gave a small sigh.

If I didn't know better, I'd swear I was falling in love with the man, she whispered to herself.

After a difficult day, Jess was relieved to have something to look forward to. Though she tried to look at it as a sort of business meeting, she couldn't help hoping that it could lead to something more. She resolved to try to draw him out this time, get him to tell her about his private life. If there really was another woman in his life, she needed to know before she made a total idiot of herself.

Her mother would have been horrified that she could even think of throwing herself at a man, as she would have phrased it. How often had she tried to explain that things were different nowadays. Women took charge of their own lives and certainly didn't always sit around metaphorically waiting for someone to ask them to dance. Poor Mum. She may have been a child of the Sixties, but escape from convention had never quite reached their corner of the world.

With a guilty pang, she realised she had never called back home. It was too late now. She didn't have enough time before Ben was due to collect her. She wanted there to be no chance of him seeing her grotty little flat and being put off by the squalor. She really must find somewhere decent to live, as soon as she had the time.

After a rather average meal and mediocre coffee, Jess tried to pump Ben for a few details about himself. Despite her intentions, she didn't seem able to come right out and ask him if he had a woman in his life. His mother's slightly genteel good manners must have rubbed off on him and such questions did not seem appropriate. In fact, she realised, it was partly his good manners that contributed to his attractiveness.

'So,' she began, 'who or what is it that keeps you in London? You said your mother would like you to move down here.'

'Oh, this and that. Business mostly. Though, as I was hinting once before, ease of communication may make that less necessary in future. It seems to have been working quite well during this stay. Once a week or fortnight in London may suffice.'

She questioned him as thoroughly as she dared without being too intrusive. Who looked after his office? Did he have other colleagues? What did he like to do for entertainment? All she managed to get from him was that he had a devoted secretary who'd been with him for years and that he worked out twice a week at a local gym. She felt no nearer knowing about him at the end of it.

Instead, he knew that there was no-one special in her life, she had a sick mother and he knew every detail of what music she liked, every film she'd seen in the last five months and that she was keen to stay here in Cornwall. What was it about him that managed to get her pouring out her entire life story while she learned nothing of him?

'I'm sorry,' she said at last. 'Rabbiting on like that. You must be bored silly by me.'

'Not at all. It's very refreshing to meet someone who isn't constantly trying to impress me with how witty they are or how suitable my mother thinks they are as a match. Well, maybe they don't say it quite so blatantly.'

Jess laughed, knowing she desperately wanted to tell him how eminently suitable a match she would be. He continued.

'Maybe we should go to the cinema

one evening. I haven't been in years. It might make a nice change.'

'Great,' Jess agreed. 'There're several good things around at the moment.'

'Name one and we'll go and join the queue one evening.'

'Oh, you can book it, by e-mail, text or phone, then pay by credit card and pick up the tickets when you get there.'

'You've lost me. I may use the phone and e-mails but text? I don't think I can do text.'

'You old-fashioned thing.' She giggled. 'Pass me your mobile and I'll demonstrate.'

He watched as her fingers nimbly skipped over the buttons and she sent a message to her own phone. He pursed his lips, peering over her shoulder so she could feel his breath against her cheek. She caught a whiff of a discreet after-shave and wondered how she could continue to keep him this close to her.

'I think I may have to stick to my computer and actual speech. I haven't got the patience or ability to do all that. Think I might need my eyes testing, too. How can you even see it?'

'OK. Text messages are out. But seriously, I'd love to go to the cinema. Name the day and I'll book it. My treat. You've bought so many meals for me, it's the least I can do.'

'I must be paying you too much if you can make such offers.'

'You haven't actually paid me at all,' she said. 'You wanted to reduce the overdraft, I think you said.'

'Oh, no,' he burst out. 'I've really been neglecting things, haven't I? Right, first thing tomorrow, we settle down to the accounts. We'll have a grand sort out.'

'Tomorrow's Saturday. We could be busy.'

'Sunday then. If you don't mind, of course. Come over for lunch. We'll spend the morning working and then we can eat and continue afterwards, if we need to. I'll order something in so you don't have to cook.'

As Jess walked up the stairs to her flat, her heart was singing. A whole day with Ben. They would be working together and discussing the future maybe. It was a good prospect.

5

By Saturday afternoon, Andrea had joined the team. She was one of several applicants for the part-time job advertised on the neatly-printed card attached to the door. Andrea seemed ideal. She was a young mother whose child had started full-time school and this would fit ideally with her day. During holidays, if they were looking that far ahead, her mother would have the little boy.

She was to start the following Monday. Demelza eyed her suspiciously and took her off to a corner, demanding a pot of tea to accompany them. Jess obliged, though knowing that she might regret it later, if her unhelpful assistant were to be in charge of her new, or rather Ben's new employee. The pair sat conspiratorially in their corner and Jess caught odd words like bossy, demanding, setting her cap at the boss's son and knew that she was being talked about to her detriment.

She shrugged. So be it. Once alone with Andrea, she would soon set her straight about things and if she didn't like it, well, there were others around who could do the job.

At last it was time to lock the door and clear up for what was left of the weekend. If things were to go on at this pace, she would need to organise afternoons off for Demelza and possibly for herself. She had time for very little other than work.

Saturday evening and nothing planned, she thought gloomily. But, she had Sunday with Ben to look forward to. She dreamed a little as she sat in her flat with only a bottle of wine for company. Impulsively, she had picked up the bottle at the supermarket when she looked in for something for supper. She'd settled for a frozen meal, too weary to cook anything and it was warming in the tiny oven provided.

She picked up the phone to call her parents, still feeling guilty that she was neglecting them. There was no reply. Even the answering machine was switched off. It was most unusual. Due to her ill-health, her mother rarely went anywhere and her father would never leave her, especially not in an evening. Concerned, she switched off her phone.

She called several times but there was still no reply. Her concern grew as she realised that she was committed to staying where she was for some time yet. No way could she let down everyone at this stage, especially after all her promises and plans. But her mother came first. If she had to go and visit her parents, she would have to drive up after closing next weekend and return overnight the following day. It was far from ideal but maybe there was a simple explanation.

★ ★ ★

Jess worked with Ben all Sunday morning, attempting to get the accounts sorted into a more easily managed order. With his mother's sudden illness, things had been neglected. He had been making some attempt to keep things straight for a long time but his mother's unique methods of paying from the till made everything very complicated. He also admitted that he had been subsidising the business for some months now. Ben hoped the café could become more than a simple hobby for his mother. Her occupational therapy, as he called it.

'You're a kind man,' she said impulsively.

'Not really. My mother is a very special lady. I wanted her to be happy. It really kept her going after my father died, and I could afford it. Besides, any mum is a one-off, isn't she? You have to make the most of them because you never know how long they'll be there. I learned that after my father's sudden death. I suppose I never spent enough time with him and then it was too late.'

Jess nodded, feeling desperately guilty suddenly.

'Look, do you mind if I call my parents?' she asked. 'Only I tried them last night and they weren't in.'

He nodded and she dialled the number. There was still no reply.

'Maybe they've gone away for the weekend,' he suggested, seeing her anxious face.

'They don't do that. Mum's unwell and always stays at home.'

'We can always close for a day or two, if you think you should go and visit.'

'Thanks, but I shouldn't panic. There's probably a good reason for it. Maybe the phone's out of order.'

He leaned over and dialled services.

'Here. Report it,' he commanded as he handed the phone back to her.

She did so, but there was nothing apparently wrong.

'No use worrying,' she said brightly. 'Let's get back to work.'

He stared at her for a few moments, put a comforting hand over hers and smiled reassuringly.

'If you're sure.'

She nodded and he pulled the books towards himself.

'If we are to make it into a proper paying business, we need to get things on to a realistic footing. Now, you were talking about a wholesaler. Did you get a decent deal?'

'Not entirely. But I needed someone local to deliver and there only seemed to be the one place. It's certainly cheaper than stocking up at the local store. When I saw what Demelza was charged for the stuff she bought in, well, I'm not surprised your mother was making a loss. I got twice that amount for the money at the wholesaler.'

They ate delicious hot pizza for lunch, delivered by the local shop.

'Sorry it's not really a Sunday lunch but there's not much alternative in this place.'

'It's delicious, really. But maybe

that's yet another avenue to explore. Home-cooked meals ready to serve. Holiday-makers might love it.'

'Brilliant idea. But it needs to be relatively inexpensive and easy to heat and serve. Look into it, will you?'

'It would take investment and a lot of new equipment.'

'Or second-hand. There are always hotels and such closing down. The local paper is always full of adverts for all sorts of stuff.'

He paused and gave a small sigh.

'Trouble is, Mum's never likely to give in and hand over the reins. It's virtually her life, what she cares most about.'

'Apart from you. You are her only son, after all.'

'I simply don't think she is ever going to be well enough to take the pressure again. She may have been very slow in her attitude to it. Laid-back perhaps. But the small amount she was doing would probably be too much for her in future. You have proved that with proper management, it can make a profit. Even in the short time you've been here, the takings have almost trebled and that's on top of the increased expenditure. You've got the right flare for it and can provide what's necessary in the available market-place. I think we need to bide our time with my mother. Let's see what happens. Now, how about another glass of wine? And what about that cinema trip you mentioned? Any objections to going on a Sunday?'

It turned out to be a rather boring film in the end, but they seemed to have enjoyed each other's company, Jess consoled herself. Ben put a nonchalant arm around her shoulder as they walked back to the car. They fitted together easily and walked together as though they were a couple. She glanced at him to see if he was reacting in any obvious way to their closeness but he looked miles away. He kissed the top of her head casually, as he held the car door open for her.

Desperate though she was to respond, she felt the need to hold back. If he kissed her again, however perfunctory it may have been, she would ask him if he really was unattached. He was driving her back to her road when they both remembered her car was still parked at his mother's house.

'Sorry, but I'll need it tomorrow, unless you intend collecting me at the crack of dawn.'

'You could always stay over.'

'I couldn't possibly,' she stammered, blushing furiously.

'Oh, sorry. That must have sounded dreadful. No, I meant you could stay here, in the spare room. Mum always keeps the bed aired and it would mean we could have another drink.'

Jess fought a small battle inside. If she asked him now about his love life, it would sound even worse, as though she was actually trying to push him into something.

'Thanks. It's kind of you but I should

get back. It may not be much but it is my place. I shall have to think about moving though. It's not exactly luxurious. All the same, thanks again. I'll see you tomorrow.'

'I'll call in at some point. I want to go to the hospital first thing. See Mother's doctors. Thanks for today, Jess. I enjoyed it. Even if it was largely work. I think we make a good team, don't you?'

'Great,' she agreed, her heart pounding.

He was standing close again, his hand under her elbow in a most familiar way. He leaned down to kiss her, this time on the lips. She kissed him back, wondering if the action was doing to him half of what it was doing to her. He pulled her towards him and held her for a few moments.

'Ben . . . I . . . Ben. Please.'

'I'm sorry. I don't know what came over me. I'm so sorry, Jess. You just looked so lovely standing there. We've been working so well together, I guess I just forgot myself. Please say you forgive me.'

'There's nothing to forgive. I wanted it, too. Very much. Only, well . . . '

'Well what?'

'Demelza says you're almost engaged, that you have a lady-friend in London.'

'It seems Demelza knows more about me than I do. I wonder where she got that idea from.'

'Your mother told her, evidently.'

'My mother?' he exclaimed. 'She knows nothing. I mean I never said a word to her. She's speculating.'

'But is there someone you see?' Jess asked.

'I have friends, yes, but there's no-one special, not in London. I'd hardly be spending time with you, would I, if there was a lady-friend languishing in London?'

'I suppose not. I'm sorry. I just thought we were being business colleagues. You took me by surprise, that's all.'

'And was it a nice surprise or a nasty one?' he asked with a glint of mirth in his eye.

'Very nice, actually. But I must leave now. Thanks again for today. I really enjoyed it all.'

Her heart was singing with joy as she drove home. He'd stood at the door watching her, as she left him. It was too dark to see his expression but she sensed he was not displeased with himself. Now she knew for certain he was not attached, she could relax and allow her feelings for him to develop.

'Just take things calmly,' she ordered herself. 'Don't rush into something you might regret.'

Before she went to bed, she tried her parent's number one more time. She was beginning to be worried all over again but there seemed nothing sensible she could do. There was no-one else she could phone and it was much too far to drive there. She tried to comfort herself with the thought if anything had gone wrong, she would certainly have been contacted by the police or other emergency services.

She slept fitfully, dreaming strange dreams and felt distinctly unrested the next morning. She made one last attempt to call her parents, before driving to Margaret Slater's tea-room to start another week.

Once more, there was no sign of Demelza. With a sigh, Jess went to organise the chairs and set the tables. The floor could have done with an extra clean but there simply wasn't time.

The baking was almost ready to come out of the oven and the first customers would be arriving soon. Until Andrea arrived, it was up to Jess to manage the cooking, waitressing and everything else that was needed. The shop bell rang and it was time for business.

'No Demelza today?' one of her first customers asked.

'I'm afraid not. You'll have to put up with me.'

Jess smiled pleasantly and took the order.

'Poor woman. She's a martyr to her headaches. Suffers so badly, poor thing. Puts on a brave face though, doesn't she?'

'I suppose she does,' Jess replied. 'I'll go and organise your coffee. A piece of shortbread with it, did you say?'

The woman nodded and Jess went into the back.

Oh, no, she realised, she had forgotten to put on the electric boiler! She put a kettle on for speed and filled and switched on the boiler. Luckily, they were not too busy as it was a Monday and many folks stayed at home to follow the traditional washday routine.

By the time Andrea arrived at eleven-thirty, Jess had caught up a little and had organised various items for the lunches. Business was reasonably brisk and one or two of the local business folk had started to frequent the tea-room for a light lunch. Jacket potatoes and various fillings had become a best-seller and were minimal effort. By the time Ben arrived, things were slowing down.

'How are things?' he asked. 'No Demelza again?'

'She didn't phone in or anything. I assume she's being a martyr to her headaches again. Poor, brave woman,' Jess said with heavy sarcasm. 'Sorry. That was uncharitable. How did you get on with your doctors?'

'All right, I suppose. It seems Mum will have to take things easily for some weeks, if not months. I tried to tell her to give up thinking of working here again but she wouldn't listen. Seems to think that Demelza will carry the business almost single-handed. Maybe it's time for you to make another visit and put her straight.'

'She'll just think it's sour grapes if it comes from me, or that I want to take over.'

Ben grinned at her but she gave a warning glance towards Andrea who was busy clearing the tables and stacking the dishwasher.

'How's it going?' Ben asked, crossing over to her.

'Fine, thanks. I've enjoyed it. I hope it's OK for me to stack the machine. Only Demelza said it was your territory and you got annoyed if anyone tried to muscle in. Only you seemed rather busy and I had nothing else to do.'

' 'Course it's all right. Just what I would have wanted. Demelza was determined not to use it and so left it to me.'

Jess was relieved to have the help she needed and would have welcomed any little thing Andrea could do.

'Now, there are a couple of potatoes left. Would you like one for your lunch? It's a bit late, I know, but you might as well enjoy the lull. We may never get another.'

As nothing had been heard from Demelza, they agreed that Andrea should come in early the next morning and take over the sick woman's chores.

If she did show, they'd simply use the time for some of the routine work. Andrea could even take over a bit of the work in the kitchen if she had nothing else to do.

Jess immediately felt better. It would give her time to look into some different lines for the meals and to do some work on any possible expansion they might plan for the future. It was an exciting prospect, assuming Margaret could be made to hand over.

'Do you mind me asking,' Andrea said after Ben had left, 'but are you and Ben, well, are you together?'

'Not exactly. We're friends though. Go out a bit together. But I haven't known him for very long.'

'He's rather gorgeous, isn't he? I wouldn't blame you setting your cap at him. Oh, sorry. That's what Demelza told me. I don't think she approves.'

'She doesn't approve of anything much. But, I must remember she's a very good friend of Mrs Slater's. Been with her since the beginning, I gather.

Take no notice of me, I'm just tired. Didn't sleep very well. You'd better get off. Your little boy will be out of school soon. Thanks very much for your help. See you in the morning. As early as you can manage.'

Disappointingly, Jess saw no more of Ben that day. He'd suggested that she might visit the hospital again but no more had been said. She cleared up and locked the door. Anyone else wanting tea or food this afternoon, would have to go elsewhere. If they ever did make it into a full-blown restaurant, they'd have to do something about more staff. She couldn't work all day and evenings as well, not long term at any rate.

She paced along the length of the room and worked out how many tables could be fitted into the space if they expanded. There was a reasonable-sized garden at the back where she'd thought they might put a terrace. A few plants and some walls to make different levels and it could be quite delightful. They might put a glazed roof over it to provide shelter while still giving the impression of dining outside.

She went out to look at the possibilities. She glanced over the wall at the shop next door. The back garden there was a total wilderness, nothing more than a dump for old junk. Maybe they would consider selling it. That would certainly make all the difference. Excited at the prospect, she left the tea-rooms, locking the doors and checking carefully that everything was turned off.

She walked to the front and looked in at the neighbouring shop. It called itself an antique shop but in reality was nothing more than a junk shop. They had a few shabby pieces of furniture and a load of small pieces, broken china and piles of old books. She had rarely seen customers in there and the owners were inclined to open when the mood took them. The building itself seemed sound enough and it would virtually double the present available space.

With this place and the tea-rooms

together, they would really have scope for business. The idea for ready-meals would necessitate a large preparation area and a large chiller and possibly freezer. Storage space would be needed for packaging materials as well as masses of fresh produce. Her mind whirled on.

Excitedly, she drove home and spent the evening scribbling on bits of paper and making scruffy-looking drawings. If she was to present any of this to Ben, she needed to set it all out carefully and make proper sketches. She realised at ten o'clock she hadn't eaten anything or even tried to call her parents. But she was carried along by her excitement.

She made some toast and a cup of cocoa and promised herself she would make sure she ate properly the next day.

Jess could hardly wait to see Ben to discuss her plans but she had to curb her impatience.

The following morning, Andrea arrived as promised and quickly cleaned and set out the room.

'Should I go and get a few more flowers? I gather Demelza has some deal with the florist but as she isn't here, I can easily go and collect them.'

'I suppose we do need some fresh ones. These are past their best. OK. We'd better keep up the standards. I'll give you some cash so there's no misunderstanding with the bill.'

She handed over a note and asked for a receipt. A few minutes later, Andrea returned with a large bunch of carnations.

'Oh, there's the change,' she said, handing back some coins.

'They were cheap,' Jess commented. 'Did they realise they were for here?'

'I never mentioned it. Sorry, won't they do?'

'No problem. They're fine. It's just that we usually spend quite a bit more than that.'

A seed of doubt entered her mind. Demelza had some special deal, did she? She wondered, perhaps uncharitably, exactly how special a deal it was.

She said nothing but stored the information away.

It was two more days later before Demelza reappeared at work. She looked round the immaculate room, ready to criticise but could find nothing amiss.

'I hope you are feeling better,' Jess said with only a tiny hint of sarcasm. 'Andrea's been coming in early to help out. I would have been in a dreadful mess without her.'

'She do these flowers?'

'Yes. They look nice, don't they? And they seem to last so well, these spray carnations.'

Demelza sniffed but made no comment.

'Fetch them from the florist, did she? Only Mrs Pankburn asked if everything was all right. Nobody collected our usual order this week. Had them ready for us, she did. Would have brought them round herself but she was too busy.'

'I see. I didn't realise they were

ordered. We just bought a bunch from the shop. Not expensive at all.'

Jess stared at the woman to see if she looked guilty but there was not a flicker from the impassive eyes. They began the routine of the day and she noticed that Demelza had evidently taken on the rôle of manageress and spent her time largely at the till, while Andrea did most of the work serving the customers.

'Take a break, Andrea,' Jess suggested. 'You've hardly stopped all day. Make a cup of tea or something and have a sit down. I'm sure Demelza can cope for a few minutes.'

'It's OK. I don't think she's feeling too good. She said she needed to sit today.'

'I'll have to have a few words with her. If she really is unwell, then she shouldn't be here. Not the environment for someone who is ill. It could be contagious and affect our clients.'

Jess was thoroughly fed-up with the miserable woman moaning and sighing all over the place. Mrs Slater would never have tolerated it, friend or no friend. At the end of the day, she tackled her.

'Have you seen a doctor?' she began kindly.

'No point. Nothing to be done. I just have to put up with my pain.'

After several minutes of arguing, suggesting and finally being downright rude, Jess realised she was getting absolutely nowhere.

'If you've finished, I'll be getting home now. It's well past my normal time but I never expect any overtime. I see it as part of my duty to Mrs Slater.'

Jess was so nonplussed, she said nothing. The woman had done next to nothing all day and now was trying to make Jess feel as if she was doing a favour by staying on. Angrily, Jess turned the sign to CLOSED and locked the door. In the back of the kitchen, Demelza was loading her basket with various items from the fridge.

'What on earth are you doing?' Jess burst out.

'I'm always allowed to take left-overs. Mrs Slater agreed it, on account of how I don't get much money for all my efforts. Small perks she calls it.'

'But these aren't left-overs. You've got a whole pack of fresh cheese there. And that cream is almost a new pot, and the salad is needed tomorrow. You're certainly not entitled to that. Mrs Slater never had any salads, did she?'

Grumpily Demelza put the bag of washed salad back and closed the fridge door.

'You can't say nothing. It was agreed between me and the boss. Whatever you think, she's still the boss and I'll do things the way I always have, until she tells me different. Just 'cos you think you're getting in with her son, doesn't mean you have any rights at all. It's Mrs Slater's business and I'll thank you to remember that. You've upset me so much I may not be able to get here tomorrow. And you can take that as your final warning.'

She stormed out, leaving Jess gaping in sheer amazement. Whatever Ben's mother said, she was not putting up with that sort of behaviour. It was blatant theft. She dialled Ben's mobile number and waited as it rang. He was not available. Maybe it was just as well. She shouldn't speak out of anger and in any case, maybe Mrs Slater had made some agreement about the left-overs. All the same, the woman should not take such liberties, not in Jess's book, anyway.

6

As Jess went out to her car, she realised it was a beautiful evening. She had seen very little of the area, always being too involved with working. She left the car and walked the short distance to the beach and sat looking at the waves rolling on to the sand. She recalled childhood holidays, days when her mother was fit enough to play on the beaches, chase balls, dig sandcastles. Such a long time ago. She pulled her mobile phone out of her pocket and dialled their number. To her relief, her father answered.

'Dad? At last. I've been so worried. You never go away and I've been trying and trying to reach you.'

'We went away to get some new treatment for Mum. Some new idea they are developing and your mother insisted on volunteering. We had to stay near the hospital for a few days. I wanted to let you know but she wouldn't hear of it. Thought you'd come rushing back to see what was going on.'

'Of course, I would have. Goodness, how is she now? Can I speak to her? You should have let me know.'

'She does seem to be responding well. I didn't tell you because it would have worried you and we didn't want to raise your hopes.'

Jess had a long chat with her mother and felt optimistic. It was still early days but on the whole, everything looked promising. There was more news, too. Her father had decided to take early retirement. The company he worked for had been taken over by a large syndicate and as everything would be much changed, he'd accepted the offer of a good pension and the chance to spend more time with his wife. They were also planning to move to a healthier climate.

'What, somewhere like the seaside?' Jess asked.

'We thought it might be good for me,' her mother continued. 'We're planning to make a few trips out and have a look around.'

'Why not Cornwall? I plan to stay here for the foreseeable future and probably longer. It's so lovely here. I'm actually sitting at the top of the beach, surrounded by wonderful cliffs, looking at the sea. It's just so magnificent. Why did we never come to Cornwall before?'

'I don't know, love. Maybe we'll make our trip down there. We'll let you know. But it does sound like such a good idea. I hate being so far away from you.'

They chatted a while longer and Jess was inevitably questioned long and hard about what she was doing and whom she was seeing. She just about managed to keep Ben out of the conversation. After all, she'd barely laid eyes on him since last weekend. Her mother was talking again, she realised.

'Oh, I should have said earlier. We got a letter from the solicitor today. I'm afraid Dad opened it, thinking it might need urgent attention. Your inheritance will be through in a couple of weeks. Exciting, isn't it? You're going to be very surprised when you read the letter and see just how much your uncle has left you. You're a very lucky young woman.'

Jess was indeed excited and thought of her plans to buy a new car and find somewhere decent to live, though now, she might need to invest it all in the business she was considering. It had become a much more ambitious plan than she had first thought.

All her plans and suggestions for the restaurant, as she was now thinking of it, were still simmering away inside her. She decided to call Ben again and dialled his number. This time she left a message.

'I'd like to speak to you soon about some more ideas I've had. Hope all is well with your mother. I've missed seeing you this week.'

She paused and then hung up. There was so much she wanted to say but there seemed little point in doing so, in a slightly anonymous sounding message.

She wandered along to the beach and sniffed the salt air. It felt good. The fish and chip shop was open and the savoury smell filled the air. She bought some and sat on the beach to eat them. Several families were draped over the rocks, enjoying their own evening meals.

She finished her meal and as she walked back to her car, her phone rang. It was Ben.

'Thanks for your message. Is everything all right?' he asked.

'Fine, yes. I've had some ideas and was wondering if you'd manage to speak to your mother about the restaurant yet. Tea-rooms, sorry.'

'Afraid not. I've been in London all week. I should have let you know. Some business needed sorting out.'

He covered the mouthpiece and she could hear distant muttering. He continued, 'Sorry about that. Will it wait until the weekend? I'll be back late on Friday.'

' 'Course. I need to talk about Demelza, too. Just a few problems. Thank heavens for Andrea though. She's been great.'

'OK. Well, I'll speak to you on Saturday morning. I have to go now.'

He was clearly with someone, Jess could tell. A female voice was speaking in the background. She said goodbye and switched off her phone. She stared at it as though it might give answers to many questions that burned in her mind. She felt jealous. Ridiculous! Ben might have been with a colleague or someone's wife. Who could tell? Whoever it might be, she felt jealous that it wasn't her.

She cursed herself for such irrational thoughts and drove back to her flat. The thought of spending an evening sitting there was too much and on impulse, she drove to the hospital to see Mrs Slater. If Ben wasn't there, she might be glad of a visitor. It was getting near the end of visiting hours but at least she could make a small point of contact.

'Mrs Slater? It's Jess. I came the other evening with Ben, remember?'

''Course I remember you, dear. Not totally senile yet, whatever Ben thinks.'

'Sorry. I didn't mean . . . I just thought you might not remember me.'

She found herself stammering slightly and began to wish she hadn't come.

'How are you feeling?'

'I'm getting on, but the doctor says it's going to take much longer than I thought at first. I hope you can manage the tea-rooms for a while longer. I know you have Demelza. She is such a tower of strength.'

'Er . . . yes, of course. Unfortunately, she's been unwell lately. Headaches or something.'

'Poor dear. She does suffer though it never usually stops her from coming to work. She must have been particularly bad to miss even one day.'

Wanting to move to safer ground, Jess steered the conversation towards Ben.

'You must miss seeing him while he's in London. I spoke to him earlier this evening.'

'He's got a theatre engagement this evening or he would have travelled back tonight.'

'Oh, that's nice. I didn't realise he liked the theatre.'

'Well, between ourselves, I think it's probably Claire who's the attraction. Lovely girl. An architect and very bright. Likely to go far. I have high hopes they'll make a match of it. It's time my son settled down and produced a few grandchildren before it's too late for me to enjoy them.'

Jess had ceased to listen.

Perhaps Demelza had been right about Ben all along. He was thinking of settling down. Her heart was plummeting and she felt a sick dread in the pit of her stomach. She'd virtually been throwing herself at him, ever since he'd said there was no special woman in his life. He'd lied to her. Why had she believed him? They chatted idly for a while longer. Then to her relief, the visitors' bell rang and it was time to leave.

'It was very kind of you to come, dear. Give my regards to Demelza and say she's welcome to visit me any time.'

'I think Ben was anxious that you shouldn't be upset by talk of work. But, I'll certainly pass on your good wishes when she comes back to work.'

'But how are you managing without her? It must be very difficult for you.'

'I'm fine. I have a friend who's coming to help out,' she lied, 'just until things are back to normal. And, of course, the new dishwasher helps enormously. Gets everything so beautifully clean.'

'That's good. Lucky you knew someone, isn't it?'

Jess's thoughts were in more of a turmoil after the visit. Instinctively, she hated Claire, whoever she was. Clever . . . intelligent . . . architect, of all things. She imagined some sleek blonde, impeccably dressed, with manicured nails and perfect make-up. Her own dark tresses were still caught back in an elastic band and her hands were positively wrecked from working. As for make-up, that was something she rarely had time for these days. Her jeans looked scruffy and the old T-shirt was the coolest thing she had to wear under her chef's overalls.

Time for a bit of pampering, she told herself. If she was to compete with some other woman from London, she needed to pull herself together before she saw Ben again. Mind you, it might already be too late. If his mother was telling the accurate truth, they were about to become engaged. She gave a shudder as she realised they could be getting engaged at this very moment.

She went into the flat and looked around. The dreary place exactly matched the way she was looking and feeling. She ran a bath and poured the last of her bath salts. The fragrance filled the room and she sank into the hot water to soak away the cares of the day. She washed her hair and experimented with styles before the steamy mirror. As always, it flopped where it wanted to go. Maybe she should get it cut short. Worth considering. At least she might try to look a little more sophisticated.

She needed new clothes and a new flat for starters. That would do her self-esteem a bit of good. Then she came back to reality. If Ben was busy getting engaged, there was no point to any of this. Did she actually want to live in this area? It was fine for holidays but for ever? Maybe she should revise her plans and set about finding herself somewhere else entirely. Another start. Another place.

She'd been told that her inheritance would be coming through soon so she would be able to buy exactly what she wanted. With a new resolve, she made some cocoa and went to bed early with a book for company.

They closed early the next day. Trade was slack during the afternoon and Jess was determined to buy herself something new to wear. If nothing else, it might cheer her up and make her feel better about herself once more. She'd been using the excuse of being too busy for too long.

There was a limited choice of shops without driving to Truro and it was much too late for that. She found a neat trouser suit and a couple of T-shirts in a local shop and also discovered she had lost weight, fitting into something a whole size smaller than usual.

Ben breezed into the café during the morning rush, looking around with interest. There seemed to be a wider age range among the clientele these days, many more younger people frequenting the shop. The wholesome looking cakes and the cookies stuffed with dried fruit and nuts were selling well and there was a cheerful atmosphere in the place. It seemed more lively than usual. Andrea was all smiles and efficiently dealing with orders and collecting money, while Jess was keeping everything flowing smoothly from the kitchen. He smiled and nodded at everyone and went into the back.

'All going well today,' he remarked. 'No Demelza again?'

'She's been off since . . . well, most of the week. She came in one day but it was all too much for her. Fortunately, Andrea's more than capable. Thank heavens we managed to find her. She's been working long hours, too, making up for Demelza.'

'We need to talk. There's so much to tell you. I phoned Mum and she's coming on well. Oh, I gather you called in at the hospital, too. How was that?'

'Fine. I trod on eggshells so as not to worry her. I was only there a few minutes, really.'

She wanted to continue that it was

long enough to learn that he was lying to her the other day. She swallowed the words back.

'Thanks. That was good of you. Shall we eat out somewhere this evening? I'm going to the hospital now, so I shall be free later on.'

'OK, if you've nothing better to do.'

In some ways, she preferred not to be alone with him so she could put off learning that he had become engaged. On the other hand, she really wanted, needed the chance to talk.

'Is there anything wrong?' he asked. 'You seem a bit out of sorts.'

'I'm fine, really. Just concentrating on my sauce.'

She stirred vigorously, beating the cheese sauce to a glossy consistency.

'What's that for?' he asked with interest.

'Lasagne. Usually goes pretty well. I'd really like to get some individual dishes and make single portions. Looks better and certainly would make life easier.'

'We'll think about it. I'm still not really sure what's going to happen long term. I don't want to spend money needlessly. Not just at present. See how things are going to pan out. I'll pick you up around seven if that's OK.'

'Thank you. That would be lovely,' she replied on autopilot. 'Oh, shall I pay Andrea out of the till? Only she's been working her socks off every day. I don't want to leave it any longer than necessary.'

'That's fine.'

She glanced wistfully through the window as he strode along the path. He was everything she liked in a man only now she knew he was taken. All the same, she could enjoy his company while he offered it even if there was no future in it.

'So, tell me what's been going on. You said there was a lot to talk about, so begin talking,' Ben said as they sipped cold wine in a new, smart restaurant later on.

'Don't know where to start. Do you

want the mundane or some of my new wilder ideas?'

'Better do mundane first.'

She brought him up to date with various things, deciding in the end that she shouldn't speak about Demelza's evident misdeeds, at least not until she had some proof and had clarified the arrangements his mother had made.

Though the conversation flowed easily, Jess felt the shadow of Claire hanging over them both. She began to tell him about her ideas regarding the shop next door to his mother's café and how she thought it could be incorporated to make a large restaurant.

'I looked over the fence and peered inside the shop. I think it would make all the difference. Your mother owns her half outright, doesn't she?'

Ben nodded.

'Well, if we could persuade them to sell directly, without involving estate agents or anything, I reckon we could manage the conversions at a reasonable cost.'

He looked excited and began to make notes on the table napkin. Discreetly, the waiter brought him a pad of paper. Jess giggled.

'Good job he doesn't know what we're talking about. We might be rivals one day. Maybe he wants to trace your writing from the bottom page so he can sabotage our plans.'

'That's better. You look less tense. I do hope nothing is really wrong,' he said, leaning over the table and taking her hand.

She pulled it away as if she had been stung.

'I'm sorry. There is something else bothering you, isn't there? Come on, tell me. What is it?'

' 'Course not. It's nothing. I expect I'm tired. End of the week and all that. Oh, did I say? My mother's been for some new treatment and is making good progress. They plan to come down here for a visit and may even move to Cornwall when my father retires.'

'That's great. It also means you're

serious about staying here yourself. I'm making similar choices, too. I think it's time I got out of London, find a nice place and settle here.'

He stared at her for a reaction and she coloured and looked away. She remained silent.

'Shall we go and take a look at next door? Tomorrow?' he asked.

'If you like.'

There was no point being despondent and she did her best to recover her usual enthusiasm. Besides, it meant she would be able to enjoy the exquisite torture of Ben's company, believing he had given his heart to another.

He made no further attempts to touch her at all, for which she was both relieved and disappointed at the same time. Not even a peck on the cheek, she thought sadly, though she knew it was her own fault. It would have been wrong, even if he had wanted to do it.

They met at the café the next morning. They walked round appraisingly and peered over the wall next door. They'd already knocked at the door, but as expected, there was no-one there on a Sunday morning. Peering through the grimy window, they could see the shop was really one large room with some storage areas at the back. They could easily knock the wall through from their place so it couldn't have been better positioned.

'We do need to put a business plan together. Cost everything properly. Project figures, turnover and such like,' Ben said.

'That sounds like a lot of work. I wouldn't know where to start.'

'Fortunately, I do. We can make a start on the basics right away and then see how it could work out in the broadest sense. I'll really have to see about discussing it with my mother first, of course, but I think she may be coming round to the idea, slowly.'

'She could always help at front of house. Man the tills, organise the seating of customers, and such.'

'Brilliant idea. She'd love that and it

wouldn't be too taxing. Maybe I should talk to her right away. This afternoon?'

'Don't rush anything. We don't want to let her worry unnecessarily. Let's see if the people next door are willing to sell first.'

'I think you're quite brilliant, Jessica Davis.'

He caught her up in his arms and danced around the scruffy little garden with her. He stopped and kissed her gently.

'No, don't say a word. I don't want to hear any protests. I simply needed to kiss you then.'

Jess obediently said nothing. Her heart was beating much too fast for speech.

7

'I assume you'll need to organise a bank loan for your share of the money,' Ben said a few days later.

He'd made a start on his business plan and was already feeling apprehensive about the costs involved.

'If so, we need at least a simple version of the business plan to be ready. We're talking about quite a large investment, even for half of it.'

'No. I already have some money, or will have soon. I was going to buy a new car actually but that can wait.'

'We're talking about a heck of a lot more than the cost of a car here,' he said doubtfully. 'I don't know quite what you were planning on, but it's going to cost thousands and thousands if we do what we were talking about.'

'That's OK. Maybe I was planning on buying a very expensive car,' she said with a wicked grin and he raised an eyebrow curiously.

'And where did you get that sort of money? Not on tips from this place, I'm sure.'

She hardly looked or acted like the daughter of some extremely wealthy family. She ignored him and continued.

'But we still need the plan, don't we? The owners of the shop next door seemed quite interested in selling, didn't they? Mind you, it's all in a pretty poor condition. Needs a heap of work doing.'

'I've got an architect coming to look it over next weekend. And I've organised a valuation of the property to be done. The surveyor is going to look in the next day or two. Oh, and Mum's coming out of hospital later today. Can't think how I forgot to mention that one.'

'That's terrific.'

She felt genuinely pleased that Margaret Slater was sufficiently recovered to go home, even though it may complicate their own plans. Then Ben's words hit her. Architect? She certainly knew of an architect among his acquaintances, and she was actually coming down to Cornwall, was she? It could be only for one reason, she supposed. She tried to swallow the bitter disappointment in her throat. What had sounded like supposition on his mother's part was now being confirmed.

It seemed ironic that she had kept silent about her money, as her father had suggested so that she didn't attract the wrong sort of man. And now it didn't matter anyhow. But Ben was a successful businessman who would never have been interested in her money anyway.

'So, all we need now is for my mother to agree to let us develop the business into something worthwhile.'

'Good luck,' Jess said as calmly as she could.

'I guess I'll need it. Still, I feel sure that we have a first-class idea here.

Selling ready-made food to tourists is an added inspiration. I can't see my mother fighting it. She's so pleased to be coming home, I think she'd agree to almost anything.'

He turned to go through the front of the café and almost fell over Demelza who had decided to come into work for once.

'Goodness, I had no idea you were there,' he said.

'Just doing my job,' she said curtly. 'What I'm paid for, or what I should be paid for. Maybe I should mention that I haven't been paid for a couple of weeks. She,' she said and jerked her thumb in Jess's direction, 'doesn't seem to realise that people actually need their wages to live.'

'I suppose it was because you haven't been into work. She could hardly have posted it to you, now, could she?'

Demelza gaped at his harsh words and was about to retort when she thought better of it.

'I'll see you get something by the end

of the day. Now, you'll have to excuse me. I have to collect my mother from hospital.'

He left the shop, concerned that Demelza had overheard their conversation. He had no idea how long she'd been standing there.

By the time he had driven his mother home from hospital, she was totally exhausted and wanted nothing more than to rest in her own room. He knew he could never bother her when she was in this state and left the discussion about the business till later. He had work to do and she needed to rest.

Leaving her with the housekeeper, who promised to call if he was needed, he went to a meeting. He called at the café on his way back home, to report the latest news to Jess. She was finishing clearing up and seemed a bit cross.

'Just that woman getting to me again. Needed to leave early for some unspecified reason. Left me with all the cleaning to do, just when I could have done without that as an extra. Her first whole day at work for weeks and she has to leave early. Sorry, I shouldn't be moaning. What is it?'

Ben's face had taken on an anxious look.

'I bet I know where she's gone. She must have overheard us talking this morning. There's every chance she's gone to stir things with my mother. Excuse me, I need to go.'

He dashed out and Jess watched him drive away as if he was being chased by the very devil himself, but he was too late. By the time he reached home, Demelza had already left and his mother was sitting up in bed looking angry and very pale and ill.

'How could you, Ben? Plotting behind my back like that. Close down my lovely tea-rooms without telling me? I realise I've been a terrible nuisance to you these weeks but I love that place. You know how much it means to me. I've put so much into it. Now you want to close it and build some sort of takeaway food shop. I thought there was more to that girl than met the eye. Thank heavens you are practically engaged to Claire or she'd be trying to entice you into marrying her.'

'Mother, calm down. You've got everything wrong. And what on earth do you mean about Claire? Honestly, I simply don't understand your mind. Now, lie back and rest, or you'll be back in hospital quicker than you can think. Whatever Demelza has told you, she has got it wrong. I didn't want to talk anything through until you are feeling better. She's a total pain, that woman. I really think she should go.'

'Of course she won't go. I couldn't sack her. Not after all this time. She's been such a good friend to me.'

'Not so's you'd notice,' Ben muttered.

'Besides, she was only doing as she was told. I said very clearly that I wanted her to keep me informed about everything that is going on. That's what she was doing. And by all accounts, it's your protégée you should be more concerned about. I suppose you are aware that she's been helping herself to money from the till.'

'Jess? Don't be silly, Mother. She wouldn't do that. She's got money of her own, anyhow.'

'So she lets you think. If she really has got money, why would she be working so hard to run my little business?'

'Mum, listen to me. Jess is completely honest. I don't know why she works so hard. Maybe she has something to prove to herself. But you must know your business has never made any money since it was opened, not until Jess took over. We're showing the first decent profit, ever.'

'I don't understand.'

'I've been subsidising it for years. I should know. I've been doing the books.'

'I don't believe you. Now, if you're going to carry on making wild accusations, I'll simply have to return to work myself and get things running properly again. Another day or two and I shall be at the tea-rooms. Then your Jess can get back to wherever she came from. Oh, and who is this friend of hers, the one in cahoots with her? Andrea, is it? Demelza has been telling me all about her. Lazy good-for-nothing, it seems.'

Ben bit back his retort.

'There's no point to any if this, Mum. That woman has spread her poison and there's nothing I can do about it. If you choose to believe her lies, rather than your own son, so be it. I'll be working in the study for the rest of the day.'

'I'll want to see the books tomorrow. Check for myself exactly what's been going on,' she called after him. 'I mean it. Bring them here or I shall go and collect them myself.'

Angry beyond words, he called Jess and told her the news. Naturally, she felt very upset and actually began to develop feelings of actual hate for Demelza. If that woman had scuppered all their chances of making a successful business, she might as well return to her own home right away. There must be other, probably even better places to start up a business.

As for Ben himself, she knew she'd lost any chance of gaining his love. Sadly, she wandered aimlessly along the beach, trying to make herself dislike the place. It had already come to mean too much to her, as if she had come to her real home at last. And it wasn't just because of Ben, she tried telling herself.

She was cheered up a little when her parents phoned to say they were coming down at the weekend. At least that meant that she didn't have to sit around watching Claire doing the plans and spending time with Ben.

'That's great. I'll book you into the hotel and try to collect some estate agent details. We can spend Sunday looking at anything suitable.'

First thing next day, Ben arrived to collect all the books and latest figures, receipts and bills from the café.

'I might as well let her go through

everything as lie there worrying. Honestly, I could murder that Demelza woman. What does she think she's doing? Is that everything?'

'I think so. You've got a heap of receipts and the till rolls but we didn't actually balance everything at the weekend. We were too busy doing the other plans. I never thought your mother would insist on seeing everything right away.'

'Don't worry about it. You've already done far more than you needed.'

It was late that afternoon when Margaret summoned her son to her room. She had a triumphant look on her face and a heap of scribbled notes.

'I told you that girl was on the take. None of these receipts balance. And she's been spending a fortune on ingredients. Far more than could possibly have been used.'

'Have you balanced it with the takings? Most of that stuff is for lunches. They are very profitable. And they're going well. Increased numbers each week.'

'There are still a large number of discrepancies. Look. Here and here.'

She jabbed her finger on the various columns.

'But several of those were well before Jess even came. I think you'll find your precious Demelza might be the one to blame, unless you made the mistakes yourself. Those are the only explanations.'

'Nonsense. I don't make mistakes. And as for Demelza, she's far too loyal.'

'But, Mum . . . '

It was pointless to argue further and Ben silently collected the books and papers. He was leaving the room when Margaret called out, 'I think you should get rid of her, that Jess, and her friend as well. Demelza can carry on for a day or two, until I'm up and running again.'

He didn't bother to reply but drove angrily to the café to tackle Jess about the discrepancies his mother had found in the recent accounts. She looked away and blushed.

'What is it? Come on. I simply refuse to believe you've been cooking the books, not for such petty amounts and not if what you say about having money is true. But, there's something wrong, I can tell.'

'I didn't want to tell you without proper proof. She'll deny it all of course.'

Hesitantly, she told him of her suspicions about Demelza, about the flower racket she seemed to have going and what was virtually stealing with taking the ingredients from the fridge.

'I'm not completely sure, as she hasn't been in much this week, but I suspect the odd bits of cash go from the till. And she's certainly pocketed all the tips that have been left. Andrea was doing all the waiting at the tables, but Demelza was sitting at the till. She had the opportunity. Andrea said she'd put any tips in the pot as usual, to be shared, as one does in catering. But there have been only a few coppers in there at the end of the day, until she was off work again. Then it changed. As for the till itself, let's say I had my suspicions. The odd fiver down when I'd thought it should be there. It's rather a difficult situation. I don't really have the authority to deal with the woman. She's obviously a friend of your mother's as well as an employee.'

Ben looked thoughtful.

'It might also explain why the takings have risen so dramatically lately. Even allowing for the lunches, as an extra, the takings are much better. But why on earth didn't you tell me before, when you first noticed it? I'm disappointed, Jess.'

She cast her eyes down and pressed her lips together. She felt tears pricking the backs of her eyes. It was so unfair to be blamed when she'd thought she was making a sensible decision. Ben continued.

'I'm not sure how to handle it though. Mother won't hear a word said against the woman. It's almost as if she has some hold over her, though that's impossible, of course. I'm simply going to have to try and keep her away from Mother. I know whenever Demelza goes to see her, she is bound to stir things up and I don't want Mum upset again. I just wish you'd told me about all of this before. Mother thinks it's you at the bottom of all this. Now it will sound like an excuse. You should have told me.'

'I'm sorry. Maybe I should have done, but I've moaned about her so much, you'd have thought I was making excuses to get rid of her.'

He went back to his home without further comment.

'But you must understand, it's serious. Jess caught her taking stuff from the fridge.'

'Of course she did. I always let her have a couple of scones and a bit of cream for her tea. Only left-overs.'

'This wasn't left-overs. Whole slabs of cheese and pots of cream. And the tips.

She never shared any of them with Jess or Andrea.'

''Course she wouldn't. I always say the tips are for her. She's the one doing the waiting at table, after all.'

'And the flowers? She pays twice as much as she should. Pockets the difference, I have no doubt.'

'A few pennies that's all. I don't begrudge her. You're just being petty. I won't sack Demelza. That's the end of it. If the poor woman needs a few extras, you shouldn't begrudge her.'

'But over the years, it must have added up to quite considerable amounts. This could be just the tip of the iceberg. I suspect she could have been taking small sums of money out of the till every day.'

'Nonsense, dear. I don't want to hear anymore. You're upsetting me. Now, I'd like a cup of coffee and you must talk to me about something pleasant. I don't want to hear another word about the tea-rooms or Demelza.'

'You really are feeling better, aren't

you?' Ben asked a little later.

'Very much, thank you. Now tell me, how is Claire? Did you enjoy the theatre the other evening?'

'She's coming down at the weekend. I've got a project she's helping me with.'

'And is that the only reason for her visit?'

'Of course. Why else would she come down?'

Margaret stared innocently at him and the penny dropped.

'Oh really, Mum. Claire is engaged to someone at her office, happily settled. Besides, I'm not interested in her as anything more than a friend, so no more matchmaking.'

'I suppose it wouldn't have anything to do with my tea-rooms, this project, would it?' she asked suspiciously.

'I thought I wasn't to mention them again.'

'Come on. You might as well tell me everything. Though I think I know what you want to do.'

Ben seized the opening and enthusiastically told her all about the plans. He suggested that she would be of great help and added the final cherry on the cake by saying that he was planning to move down to Cornwall personally, to help with the organisation of the project. He told her he'd had enough of living in London.

'You seem to have it all planned. It sounds wonderful, darling. And to think you'd live here, well, that settles it, doesn't it? Do whatever you want with my little business. I'm really too weary to fight you any more. Besides, the thought of going back to baking hundreds of scones every week was not very appealing. I did enjoy the company though. Your plans sound as though I might still have a bit of company and a nice, easy little job.'

'You mean you agree? That's fantastic. I can't wait to tell Jess.'

'And would Jess also be part of your reason for staying here?' she asked innocently. 'Perhaps I'd better take another look at her.'

'Mother, you're incorrigible.'

'Oh, I see. Like that is it?'

She smiled a knowing smile and made plans to invite Jess for dinner at the first possible chance.

'So, you see, it can all start happening,' Ben said happily to Jess much later. 'Mother's agreed and we make our offer for next door. Fair price, of course, based on the surveyor's recommendations. Organise planning permission, once we've got Claire to do the plans. Actually, she'll do that for us as well. You'll like her, she's a brilliant architect and a good friend. She'll give us first-class service for a decent discount.'

'I see,' Jess said in a small voice. 'Claire, is it? She's going to be part of the project?'

'Only as far as the building part goes. You can tell her exactly how you want it done and she'll tell us if it's possible. She'll give us a special deal, better than we'd get anywhere else. Now, there's heaps to do, so cancel any plans you have for the next year or two. Slater's Tea-Rooms are about to change, big time.'

He grabbed her wrists and swung her round, almost demolishing the crockery store as he did so. She laughed at his excitement and allowed him to put his arms round her and hug her, even though she knew it wasn't right. She was about to meet his fiancée and he was hugging her.

'I'll be busy for the rest of today,' he told her, 'but we must get together this evening. I'll call you.'

The call from Margaret Slater came as a total surprise. Would Jess find the time to call at the house after work and say nothing to Ben? Puzzled, she left the café slightly early and drove to the Slaters' house.

'Gosh, you do look better,' Jess burst out without thinking.

Margaret was sitting in the pretty living-room, a tray of tea beside her.

'Thank you. I feel it. Do sit down. Can I pour you some tea?'

Jess nodded gratefully.

'I wanted to talk about your plans. It all sounds very exciting, but how on earth can you afford to buy half of the business, if I may ask?'

Jess filled her in on all the details of her inheritance, though without telling her the sum involved. Jess was still trying to come to terms with the final figures supplied by her solicitor. She could buy her new car, provide some extra help for her mother as well as invest in the business. She sent a quiet prayer of thanks to her uncle, whom she had never known.

'And Ben? You seem to have become very close in so short a time.'

Jess looked down at her fingers as the blush spread over her cheeks.

'You're fond of him, aren't you?'

'Yes,' she squeaked. 'Though you must never tell him that. It's all too late, isn't it?'

'I like you,' she said suddenly,

causing Jess to stare in surprise. 'I was all set to dislike you intensely, especially for changing my business but I think you could make us all happy. And possibly rich, too. I assume I get an interest in the business as I'm providing the premises.'

'Of course. There will be heaps of things you can do to help. Front-of-house manager for a start. And, thank you for your nice comments. But I'm not sure about the happy part. Isn't Ben getting engaged?'

'I hope so. Soon. Very soon. I want to see a few grandchildren around before my time comes.'

As soon as she had finished her cup of tea, the one that she felt might choke her at any minute, Jess made her excuses and left. She was totally confused at the changes in Ben's mother. Maybe she was more than a little confused herself, she wondered. She realised that she liked Ben's mother. Despite everything, she felt they could even become friends.

She glanced at her watch, remembering she had done nothing about her parents' visit at the weekend. She booked them into a hotel and called at the estate agents to pick up a few property details. Maybe they should just look around at this stage, decide which area they'd like to live in. There was just too much happening all at once.

To her surprise, she also liked Claire when they met. Ben drove her to the café on Saturday morning. She wasn't the ultra-glamorous, sleek woman she had been expecting but had a rather homely face and wore jeans and a large sweater. She wandered round with a pad and pencil, drawing, measuring and asking endless questions, obviously totally focussed and on the ball with her work.

'Would you like some lunch?' Jess offered, as the morning wore on.

'I'm meeting my fiancé actually. Geoff's been taking a look at the town while I was here with Ben. See exactly where our dear friend intends to bury himself. Thanks anyway. Are you joining us for dinner this evening?'

Jess was reeling from the shock of her words. Fiancé? Did that mean . . .

'I'd love to but I have my parents staying for the weekend.'

'Couldn't we all join forces? Your mother might enjoy an evening out, too, Ben. And if you two are about to become partners, the parents all need to know each other, don't they? It would be fun to meet everyone together. We shall have so much to decide and plan and it seems everyone is involved anyway.'

'Excellent idea,' Ben said happily.

'Well,' Jess began, 'as long as it isn't too much for your mother. Thanks.'

The smile on her face was radiant. She liked the sound of the word, partners. There may still be a long way to go in their relationship but now she knew that Ben wasn't engaged, who knew what might happen?

She was also greatly relieved to know

that he had not been fibbing to her. And, what was more, his mother liked her. That was a very good start to anything else that might happen.

8

Once they had seen her dreadful flat on the evening they arrived, her parents were intent on finding somewhere decent to live, where they could all share.

'How could she have lived there for so long?' they asked her.

She shrugged it off, saying she simply never got around to looking for anything else. While Jess was at work, they had spent all of Saturday driving around and had already found an area they liked.

'Don't you think you should take your time?' Jess said anxiously. 'I don't want you to rush into anything, especially not on my account.'

They took no notice and her mother continued to enthuse about the lovely little village tucked away in a deep valley that ran down to the sea.

'And there's a perfect bungalow for sale, gorgeous views and everything. Three bedrooms, too. We're going for a proper look tomorrow.'

'Looks like you hardly need my input. I hope it works out for you.'

She felt happier than she had done for a while and told them of the plans for dinner that evening. They were delighted to be meeting the man they suspected meant a great deal to their only daughter. Granted, she'd told them he was to be a business partner but her mother had her suspicions that there was much more to it than that.

'We were hoping to meet your Ben,' her mother said without a flicker.

'He isn't my Ben. So just take that look off your face and stop plotting.'

She may as well have been calling to the wind. Her father shrugged.

'I'll pick you up at seven and just behave yourselves this evening. I don't want you making any assumptions,' Jess said as she left their hotel.

She dressed carefully, despite her

limited wardrobe. She wanted to look her best for the occasion.

It was an interesting evening. Jess found Claire's fiancé to be slightly boring but they were so obviously in love that she could relax and even flirt mildly with Ben. She cast anxious glances at Margaret and her mother but they were talking non-stop. It appeared they had found a great deal in common. She grimaced slightly. Probably the pair of them were plotting about the future prospects of their progeny. It was even worse than she suspected. Once the two mothers had got together, it was obvious from the start that they had decided their off-spring needed to get together as soon as possible.

Jess saw a flicker of annoyance cross Ben's face at some of the thinly-veiled hints from his mother about the future. She said pointedly, more than once, how nice it was to see Claire and Geoff so happily engaged, but Ben grimaced slightly. Jess wondered if it was the situation between his old friend or his mother's words. Whatever it was, she knew that she herself should take care not to rush things.

Besides, he was also seeming to be rather more distant with her, once the exuberance of the initial plans for the business had worn off. Perhaps she compared badly with Claire whom she knew was close to him. Doubts about the future crept into her mind again.

After the weekend was over, things settled back to near normal. Margaret invited Jess to the house at every opportunity and it was obvious that she was matchmaking overtime.

After a couple of weeks of his mother's pressure, Ben, it appeared, had had enough.

'Look, I need to go to London for a while. A few things need sorting at my office. Nothing's going to happen here for some time so I'll get things moving from my end. You can go on running the café just as you are for now and I'll let you know as soon as the plans are ready. If I'm in London, I'll be able to check with Claire that everything we want is included. I'll send you the first drafts as soon as they're ready. Don't be afraid to make any suggestions.'

'I'll look forward to seeing the finished results.'

It had become rather tense lately and a breather would probably do them all good, however much she was going to miss seeing Ben each day. He rattled off a few details about cash and payments.

'Don't bother Mum more than you have to, though I think she'd probably like to feel she's a bit involved. I don't think she will interfere at all. If Demelza plays up again, just sack her. I don't think Mum will have any complaints on that score any more.'

'She's been fine lately. I think she may have learned some sort of lesson. I think she's realised that she might actually get the sack if she doesn't toe the line.'

Over the next couple of weeks, they were very busy. Jess felt frustrated and anxious. The plans had arrived remarkably quickly and a price agreed for the shop next door. She'd suggested a few minor changes to the plans and these had been written in. It was now a case of waiting for planning permission to be granted. In Claire's opinion, it was a foregone conclusion. Jess would have liked to share her optimism.

In desperation to focus her thoughts away from Ben a little, she bought the local paper and scoured it for adverts for second-hand catering equipment. As Ben had suggested, there was plenty around. In fact, so many places were closing down, she began to feel nervous about the whole enterprise. If others were closing, how could she think they would survive?

She marked a couple of auction sales and organised the food for the day, so that she could attend. She wanted to see the sort of prices things fetched so that they could make a more accurate assessment of the costs.

She almost felt carried away by the

tension in the air at the sale and was practically bidding for items herself, even though they were not yet anywhere near ready to begin stocking up. It might be tempting fate, she tried to convince herself as she saw absolute bargains flowing away from their doors.

A month later, her whole life had completely changed again. After a couple more visits, her parents had bought the bungalow they had liked and immediately managed to sell their own property. They were planning to move down as soon as possible so she was kept even busier as she helped sort out the final details for them.

They were getting a company to do the actual move and insisted that she needn't go to help in any way. They'd prefer her to organise the new place and she spent several evenings measuring and discussing where her parents' furniture could go.

Ben had made several visits down to Cornwall but seemed to show little interest in Jess herself. She felt slightly hurt but decided he was simply too busy re-adjusting his life. He would soon be moving down permanently, so it was probably little more than a temporary blip. When they were ready to close the tea-rooms before the work could start, he came down again.

The farewell party at the tea-rooms had been her own idea and many of the customers had come for a goodbye drink when they opened their doors for the last time. Margaret had been the perfect, charming hostess and everyone promised to come to the new restaurant when it was finished. If she felt distressed at the coming changes, she showed none of it. Even Demelza was on her best behaviour, hoping for a job in the new premises, no doubt.

Andrea was delighted to think of her own secured future when they promised her a regular job. Even Ben had seemed more like his old self. He continued to avoid spending too much time alone with her, however, except when they had business matters to discuss. She partly blamed his mother for appearing too keen, but she also wondered if he had other interests in London, perhaps. She discarded that idea as he was still intent on living with his mother for the time being.

Once the building work began, Jess was a constant visitor to the property, often to the annoyance of the builders. She carried a notepad with her at all times and was always sizing up corners for different purposes and planning where things would go. Her ideas seemed to grow larger and larger and she was already making plans for the gardens at the rear. She had moved in with her parents for the time being, insisting on paying for help in the house out of her own money. Though both parents protested, she got her own way.

'I don't know why you've become so bossy, these days,' her mother complained.

'I'm a businesswoman now. A full partner in what will be the most successful restaurant and outside catering business in the South-West. Now, I have a job for you. I'd like you to write all your favourite recipes. Oh, and all the things you have enjoyed eating at every restaurant you've ever been to.'

'You don't expect much, do you?'

All the same, it gave both parents an interest they hadn't expected and they began going out to eat at different places, just to check on what was available, they insisted. They often took Margaret with them and the two women began to spend a great deal of time together.

'She's a bit lonely with Ben away so much,' her mother explained. 'It seems only right to include her on the trips as she is a part of the whole business, isn't she, dear?'

'Of course she is, Mum. I'm pleased the two of you have become such friends. I was thinking at one time that I should find a sort of companion housekeeper for you but I don't think you need it, what with Dad being retired and Margaret always around.'

'And you living at home again. I don't know when I have ever been happier.'

'I'm glad, Mum. Very glad. But don't expect me always to be living at home. This is only temporary.'

'Oh, of course not. You'll be getting married sometime, won't you?'

'I'm going to do some work now,' Jess said, hoping to escape further questions. 'I want to design some uniforms for the waiters and maybe kitchen staff. Something eye-catching.'

Ben finally returned to Cornwall when the major building work was nearing completion. It was late October and they would soon be ready to begin equipping the kitchen and restaurant. It had long been decided that the chintzy look had to go and they'd sold the old tables and chairs and much of the kitchen equipment that was considered too antiquated to be used. Ben went with Jess to several auctions and they bought stainless steel tables, shelving units for storage and a whole range of equipment like fryers, grills and smaller pieces.

'It's all so exciting,' she told him as they drove back. 'I just love that huge set of matching pans we got.'

Ben laughed.

'You are funny. Most women would be excited by new clothes or jewellery rather than a set of pans.'

'Well, I'm not most women then. We should get the seating organised next. I still fancy some built-in benches round the outside of some of the room. What do you think?'

'I think you did us all such a favour that day you walked in and asked for a job.'

He looked at her, the softness in his eyes that she hadn't seen for some weeks. She smiled back at him.

'I think you did me such a favour when you took me on, unseen, untried.'

He reached over for her hand and gave it a gentle squeeze.

'You'd better not let your mother see

you doing that. She'd have us up the aisle and be decorating the nursery.'

She closed her eyes, wishing she'd got some control over her stupid tongue. Ben made no comment and she opened her eyes to look at his expression.

'My mother and yours combined are becoming quite a force to be reckoned with. But nobody is going to push me into something unless I want it first.'

Jess felt sick. That was telling her.

'We should discuss the plans for the final décor,' Jess said, attempting to move the subject to safer ground.

'I thought we'd already decided on white walls with bright prints, and plants. Lots of plants. Pine furniture. Green fabric for the side benches.'

'We need tables that can easily be moved together to make larger tables for groups. The plants are to provide a screen for couples wanting to be more private but they must be in easily-moveable troughs.'

'You're getting very decisive.' Ben smiled.

'My mother calls it bossy. But it all has to be done, doesn't it? Oh, and we need to line up suppliers. I want to use local produce and as much organic stuff as possible. I thought we'd have an extensive range of vegetarian dishes available. Gosh, there is still so much to do.'

Ben laughed. He was delighted to see such enthusiasm and it was brushing off on him. He may have had little to do with food, apart from enjoying meals out, but he was determined they would be successful. With Jess beside him, how could they be any different?

The two families had got into the habit of lunching together on Sundays, taking turns to visit each other's homes. As Ben had usually been away, it seemed all very new to him. He drove his mother to the Davis's and realised it provided a perfect opportunity to relax and keep everyone up to date with plans and developments.

'You know, I rather like the idea of being involved in some way myself,' Jess's father announced at the end of the meal.

'Don't be silly, dear, you know nothing about cooking,' Mrs Davis said.

'No, but he knows a lot about accounting, doesn't he?' Jess said with a glint in her eyes. 'He could maybe help you, Ben? And the ordering . . . he could help with that. He's a dab hand at getting deals and organising the logistics of deliveries and so on. If we get the outside catering and chilled meals side moving, he'd be wonderful at organising the details.'

'Are you getting a van? I'd really enjoy driving a van,' Mr Davis said enthusiastically.

'Oh really, George. You're not a van driver. Whatever gave you that idea?'

'Sounds good to me,' Ben said. 'I think we'll need all the help we can get, especially if it comes at a reasonable price.'

'I'd be glad to do it for occupational

therapy,' Mr Davis told them. 'I was never really ready to retire, if the truth be told. It just seemed like a good deal at the time. Too many things were about to change.'

'You'll be on the payroll like anyone else. Then we can fire you if it doesn't work out,' Jess said with a laugh.

'I hope you are planning on getting a chef, too,' Margaret suggested.

'I'm the chef,' Jess protested.

' 'Course you are, but not all day and every day. But seriously, we need at least one other chef, or two.'

They began another long discussion, mostly conducted by the two mothers.

'After all, we can't have the place totally reliant on Jess, can we? She might get married sometime and then there'll be the grandchildren to consider.'

Jess glared at her mother's apparently innocent remark. Ben caught Jess's hand under the table and signalled that they should leave. Silently they slipped away. They weren't there to see the two conspiratorial women nod at each other and grin. They shook hands and sent Jess's father to the kitchen to make some coffee. Outside, Ben led Jess to his car.

'If I don't escape the maternal mayhem, I shall go mad. What is it with those two? Let's go to the beach.'

Jess slipped into the seat beside him. She felt anxious, disturbed. Didn't Margaret realise that if she persisted in pushing at Ben that way, he was going to leave again? Probably for good the next time.

'I'm sorry. I've never seen my mother quite this bad,' Jess apologised.

'It must be what comes of having a beautiful daughter.'

'What me?' Jess said in surprise. 'I've never thought of me as beautiful. I'm too down to earth.'

'Come on. Race you to the rocks,' Ben challenged, as they stopped the car near to the windy beach.

Laughing together, they rushed across the beach, splashing through the pools left by the tide. Ben beat her and she arrived panting beside him.

'I must be out of condition. I should have been able to win easily,' she panted. 'All I've achieved is to ruin a perfectly decent pair of trainers.'

She bent down to poke at her squelching shoes.

'They're revolting.'

'You look gorgeous to me, with the wind tugging at your hair. Come here.'

He pulled her close and kissed her cold cheek, moving along towards her mouth. She kissed him back, feeling as if she were flying with the wind, floating high above the ground. He broke away and held her in his arms.

'Hey, watch out. The mothers may have sent spies after us.'

She spoke quickly from deep nervousness. She didn't want the moment spoiled but was too scared to move in case he let go.

'Jess, please don't say anything until I've finished. I've loved you from the moment I first saw you. I was too afraid to tell you in case you didn't feel the same way. After that first time I kissed you, I was certain. But you pulled away from me. I've tried to keep myself in check ever since then. I didn't understand, when at first you seemed to respond to me. I didn't know why you pulled away from me. Is there any chance you might one day return my feelings?'

'Oh, Ben, I can't believe this. We've both been very silly. Your mother told me you were getting engaged. She hinted it was Claire and I believed her. You were spending time with her, took her to the theatre. Then you wanted to move back to London.'

'But Claire is a friend, always has been, and Geoff was with us at the theatre. It was my thanks to them for some work they'd done for me. My mother has always had an over-active imagination. When she picked you for her next victim, I bolted, retreated back to London. I didn't want her putting you off when I hadn't even discovered if there was a chance for me.'

'Come here, silly. Of course I love you. I have loved you from the start. In fact, don't be cross, but almost the first day, I was planning our wedding.'

'So does that mean you'll marry me?'

'Yes, yes,' Jess yelled as the wind tossed away her voice. Ben laughed happily.

'What is it with you women? Wedding plans? Oh, no. Not a meringue creation of a dress and top hats for the men?'

'No. I was thinking more of a cliff top with wild flowers in my hair and several Celtic maidens dancing some strange ritual in a circle. But you could wear a top hat if you liked.'

'Thank heavens for that. But isn't it a bit windy at this time of year?'

'It was late spring when I was planning it all.'

'I see. Well, it strikes me we've wasted quite enough time already. Let's go and break the news to the powers-that-be.'

He drew her close and kissed her again.

'You know, I've been scared to talk about anything other than business lately,' he told her as they walked back to the car, hand in hand. 'I thought you'd find me too boring.'

'That's nonsense. You're a very attractive man. I was wondering if I should have a complete make-over so that you'd notice me. I did buy a new T-shirt towards it.'

'It escaped me, I'm afraid. I'm not very observant, as you must be realising. I'll try to change.'

'Don't you dare. I might have to start trying too hard. As you said, I'm not the usual woman impressed by diamonds and designer outfits.'

'You'll have to put up with one diamond, at least. Mother will insist. You can hardly wear a saucepan for an engagement ring.'

★ ★ ★

They drove back home and tried to look casual as they went in. Lunch had been cleared away and the two mothers and one father were sitting by the fire, innocently chatting as they waited.

'Have you fixed a date?' Margaret burst out immediately they were inside.

'Oh, Margaret, dear, we agreed we'd wait until they told us.'

'You see? It's hopeless,' Jess exclaimed. 'I told you it was pointless trying to do anything on our own.'

'We're engaged,' Ben said fatuously.

The two mothers clapped their hands together with a cry of, 'Yes!'

'Yes, dears, of course you are. But when's the wedding to be? Only there's such a lot to arrange.'

'We haven't discussed it yet.'

'Christmas is such a nice time for a wedding. The bridesmaids can wear red velvet and the older ones, green silk. You'll look lovely in white velvet, Jess, your lovely dark hair and all.'

'I'm not sure we can wait till Christmas. It will be too cold on our cliff top,' Ben teased. 'We want a Celtic ceremony. You know the sort of thing.

Wild maidens dancing round, flowers in their hair.'

'Now that really does sound interesting,' Jess's father put in.

The look on their mothers' faces was almost stricken.

'Don't tease them, Ben.' Jess laughed. 'But seriously, it must be a simple ceremony. No bridesmaids or silly white frock. I'd hate all that. It's marrying Ben that is important to me, not who wears the most outrageous outfit. We can always have a big party for everyone else. You can wear whatever you've been planning for that.'

Her mother and Margaret stared at her and then looked at each other.

'What makes you think we had any plans of any sort?' her mother protested.

'I know you too well. You're both as bad as each other.'

She laughed. There was a babble of conversation and Jess and Ben left them all to it once more.

'I'm adamant about this, you know. I

refuse to do the white dress bit. Besides, I want to enjoy being engaged for a while. I'm so happy, Ben.'

'Me, too. Shall we go down and look at our restaurant? We'll have to decide on a name for it. How about Slater's? Mum would like that and it would sort of continue the old name.'

'Or Davis's? That would continue my name.'

'But you'll be a Slater by the time we open.'

Jess gave a little start of pleasure. It took some getting used to, after all these weeks of wishing and longing.

They stood in the huge, empty room, dark and gloomy as the evening was falling. The bare, plastered walls were awaiting decoration. Wires stuck out of the walls where the lighting would be fixed. They went into the kitchen and stared at more empty spaces. Immediately, the ideas were pouring out from both of them and wedding plans were forgotten.

In the building that was once next

door, the cold room and preparation space was waiting. The yards at the rear had been levelled and concreted, ready to build the garden and a small area to park delivery vans.

Hand in hand, they wandered round their new restaurant, imagining the future evenings they would spend here, the room filled with diners. They had a month to get it ready for the most important occasion there would prob-ably ever be for them.

'We can do it,' Jess promised.

For the next weeks, they both worked themselves into the ground. Her par-ents gave them the greatest support possible. By Christmas week, the bright rooms of Slater's looked wonderful. They had a huge tree and discreet decorations gave the required festive appearance to the room. On December 23, Jess and Ben slipped away to the registry office and were married with only the three parents for witnesses.

Jess wore a simple cream silk suit, a gesture to the mothers. To allow for preparations, the promised party and grand opening was to take place the next day, on Christmas Eve, when the doors were to open all day for guests and customers.

'Happy, darling?' Ben asked at the end of a hectic day.

'Very. This is going to be the best Christmas ever. Every table is booked for Christmas dinner and I think James is going to prove the perfect choice as chef. He's far better than I ever could be. And Andrea will be here with her family as guests.'

'And Demelza. Mother insisted.'

'And lots of friends are coming down. I think our wedding celebrations could go on for the full twelve days.'

'And then we're going to take a break.'

He handed her an envelope.

'Plane tickets? To the Caribbean? But how can we go now?'

'It's in a couple of weeks. It's all organised. You didn't think you'd have to do without a honeymoon, did you?'

'But the restaurant. We're just starting. We can't leave at this stage.'

'You're reckoning without the mothers! Imagine what they'd say if we didn't go away. We'd never hear the end of it.'

'You're right. Bless them.'

THE END